Unplanned Love

by

Sharon C. Cooper

ISBN: 978-1-946172-15-0

Formatted By Enterprise Book Services, LLC

Disclaimer

This story is a work of fiction. Names, characters, and incidents are either products of the author's imagination or are used fictitiously. Any resemblance to actual events, locales, organizations or persons, living or dead, is entirely coincidental.

Chapter One

"I'll only consider you for the CEO position if you're married."

Charlee Fenlon stared opened mouth at her father who was sitting at the head of the boat-shaped conference table shuffling papers. Surely, she hadn't heard him right. There was no way he'd keep her out of a position that she was more than qualified for because of her marital status.

She gripped the back of one of the leather chairs in an effort to rein in the annoyance and the anger swirling within her. The more she played his words around in her mind, the harder it was to drum up some semblance of calm.

"Let me make sure I understand," she said slowly, her teeth clenched and the hold on the chair tightening. She reminded herself that at the moment, Kingslee Fenlon was her boss, not her father. "You're willing to break a number of labor laws by claiming that I'm not qualified for the CEO position because I'm not married. Is that what you're saying? Because if it is, I'm going to make a phone call that will—"

"Of course, that's not what I'm saying." He set the stack of papers that he'd been holding in his large hands onto the table, giving her his full attention. His bushy, dark brows with a hint of gray drew into a frown. "Don't twist my words."

"Are you kidding me? Dad, I didn't twist anything. Those *were* your exact words!" she yelled. Suddenly, remembering where they were, Charlee lowered her voice. The conference room door was closed, still there were a couple of offices within earshot. She wasn't sure why he worked in there instead of his office, but this was where she'd found him.

Somehow the topic of CEO had filtered into the conversation. The subject had been a course of contention between them from the moment he mentioned his plan to retire at the end of the year. This was the first time he had spewed such nonsense.

"Those might've been my words, but you're taking them out of context," he said in his usual calm tone making Charlee angrier.

Kingslee Fenlon, founder and CEO of Fenlon Manufacturing, a company that produced construction equipment and machinery parts, was always the epitome of cool. But right now, his normally refined and not easily shaken persona wasn't as unaffected as he was trying to let on. That vein in his forehead, the one just above his left brow that often popped out when he was pissed, made a bold appearance. Still, unlike her, who sometimes wore her feelings on her sleeve, he looked calm and in control.

"Yes, I want you married before you slide into that type of position," he said, going back to organizing his papers. "I want you to have a life…a happy life outside of work. Sweetheart, you're never going to have that if you spend eighteen hours a day doing something that centers around your job and this company. And that's what you're already doing as Director of Operations. What do you think will happen as CEO?"

"I know how to delegate, and I'll have even more support when I'm CEO."

"That might be so, but you have that now. Yet, you're still doing the work of two people."

He sighed and sat back in the chair, slightly rocking back and forth.

He glanced up and met her gaze. "I know you're ambitious and have been working towards overseeing the company, but there's more to life than running this business. The position is very demanding and can pull a person under in a heartbeat. Granted, I've seen some improvements with you. You're not traveling for work as much as you used to, but how often do you leave the office before eight p.m.? How often do you find yourself sitting at your desk on Saturday or Sunday, trying to do that one more thing or sign on one more client?"

Charlee broke eye contact and huffed out a breath. Instead of answering her father's questions, since he already knew the answers, she strolled to the wall of windows where sunlight poured into the room. The conference room sat several stories above ground level and overlooked a picturesque courtyard.

Practically every week, her father got on her case about letting the job be her whole life. But what did he expect? The company was thriving. A lot of that had to do with the processes that she had implemented. She came up with those ideas by having her thumb on the pulse of the operation. Unfortunately, that meant long days at work.

A boulder-like weight that Charlee hadn't felt when she first walked into the room, settled on her shoulders as she stared out of the window. The sight of the charming and peaceful looking courtyard did nothing to smooth out the irritation her father had ruffled.

Another warm July day in Cincinnati and a few people who worked for their company clearly understood the concept of getting some air. Sabrina, an HR supervisor, shed her suit jacket and strolled along the cobblestone walkway circling the large water fountain. She looked as if she didn't have a care in the world as she stopped periodically to actually smell the flowers. There was another woman Charlee didn't recognize sitting on a rod-iron bench, staring at the screen of some sort of E-reader. People milled about outside, enjoying the weather while Charlee was detained inside, getting ready to attend a meeting.

She couldn't help but think that her father was right. She had no social life. When was the last time she ate lunch away from her desk? She couldn't remember the last time she'd gone out for cocktails with friends. Or taken a trip that didn't involve work.

Outside of her career, she didn't have much of a life, at least not one she could brag about. She possessed the finest clothes, the most expensive shoes, furniture, appliances, and electronics. They filled her luxury apartment, but they couldn't fill the void in her heart.

"Are you happy?" her father asked, his voice carrying across the room.

The simple question stabbed at Charlee's already tattered nerves. At one time, she could honestly answer yes. Now, deep down inside, and during so many lonely nights, she knew something was missing.

Liam.

Liam Jenkins, her ex-fiancé.

Rarely did a day go by, especially in the last year and a half, that she didn't think of him and all that she'd given up. And now that his cousin was married to her best friend, they frequently ran into each other—a mixed blessing. It was always good to see his handsome face, but the sight of him always reminded Charlee of her biggest mistake—letting him walk out of her life.

"You're a workaholic," her father said, interrupting her thoughts. "I refuse to continue feeding into that behavior. I had hoped that when you were promoted to Director that you would be in town more and maybe even settle down.

"You might not travel as much, but the long days you put in are just as bad. How are you ever going to meet someone and have a family if you're in the office or on the road all the time? You're not getting any younger. Your window of—"

"You act as if I'm old or something," Charlee said, turning to face him. "I'm only thirty-one."

"Only? Your mother was *only* thirty-six when she died of a heart attack. I will *not* play a role in you following in Charlotte's footsteps." His words were thick with emotion, his sorrow almost palpable.

Charlee lowered her gaze and interlocked her fingers in front of her, not wanting to see the pain and loss in his eyes. She had witnessed the look countless times, like on her mother's birthday or the anniversary of when her mother and Kingslee first met.

Charlotte had died over fifteen years ago, but her father's love for her mother never ceased. To this day, he had never married. There had never been another woman to claim his heart.

For Kingslee, it had been love at first sight. Actually, for both of them, but her mother had put her career before their relationship. While living in San Antonio, they'd dated for a couple of years. Each time Charlee's father mentioned marriage, her mother put him off, asking for more time.

Kingslee eventually gave up, moved to Cincinnati, and started Fenlon Manufacturing. But during one of his visits back to San Antonio, Charlee had been conceived. Even then, her mother wouldn't agree to marry him. By that time, she was a junior partner at her law firm with an ambition to make partner before she turned thirty-five.

Charlee glanced up when she heard the crunch of wheels rolling over the hardwood floor. Her father had pushed his chair back from the table and stretched out his long legs. He folded his thick arms across his chest and studied her. Even sitting down, he was an imposing figure. In his sixties, Kingslee was over six feet tall and well built.

"I can't lose you the way I lost her, but that's exactly what's going to happen if you don't make some changes in your life," her father said quietly. "You're not getting the job, Charlee."

Her anger went from zero to sixty. "You can't do that to me!"

"I can do whatever the hell I want. It's *my* company."

"It's against the law. You can't withhold a job from me because of my marital status."

"Your personal life, or lack thereof, is not the only reason I'm *not* just going to slide you into that position. You're not ready for that type of responsibility."

"Yes, I…"

He lifted his hand, effectively silencing anything Charlee was about to say, and her hackles stood on edge.

"You're too reckless. I've watched you grow and mature over the years, but you're still impulsive. Acting first before thinking a situation through. Making decisions based solely on your gut is not going to cut it in the CEO's position. There is too much at stake for that type of behavior. I will not let you jeopardize all that we've built by acting on your whims."

Charlee glared, fighting to maintain the type of control she had mastered when things weren't going according to plan.

"I poured my life into this company with every intention of someday running the family business. Clearly, my efforts, my blood, sweat, and sometimes tears, even my innovations that have taken this company to new levels mean nothing to you."

Her father stood slowly and approached her, still maintaining a sliver of distance, assuming she would pull away if he touched her. All it ever took was one of his warm, bear hugs to wipe away any discord between them.

Not today. Today, she wasn't having any of that.

"Sweetheart, nothing could be further from the truth. You've worked for the company since you were seventeen. During those fifteen years, you learned practically every aspect of the business from manufacturing to sells. I would like nothing better than to see you run a company that I have built from the ground up. But not at the expense of you finding true happiness.

"I always have your best interest in mind. I've steered you in the right direction whenever the need presented itself, and I'm doing that now. I'm not saying that you can never be CEO, but—"

"But you don't want me to be like my mother and put my career before love."

Too late.

Charlee's heart ached at the thought. Little did he know, she had already done that and regretted it every day since. Except she wasn't her mother. At least that's what she kept telling herself.

"You don't have to respond," Charlee said, a sudden bout of sadness of her mother's death, consuming her. "I already know the answer."

A quick knock sounded on the door before it swung open.

"Mr. Kingslee, your three o'clock—" Rebecca, his assistant, words trailed off when she spotted Charlee. "Oh, I am so sorry. I didn't realize…"

Charlee didn't hear anything else Rebecca had to say. Instead, her gaze landed on the man standing next to the woman. The man she would always love. The man she had foolishly let walk out of her life.

Liam.

The anger directed at her father only moments ago slowly dissipated when Charlee met Liam's gaze. She drew in a breath as a sweet thrill spiraled through her veins. Every cell in her body came alive at his presence.

How was it possible that each time they ran into each other, her reaction was the same? Warmth traveled through her, heating womanly areas that hadn't been touched in a long time. Sure, Liam was tall and gorgeous with brooding, coffee-colored eyes, sienna brown skin, and lips that looked so darn kissable she could almost taste them from across the room.

7

And then there was his perfectly groomed, full beard that sparked something wicked within Charlee. The same, soft beard that used to gently brush the inside of her thighs whenever he…

Whoa!

Heat rose to her face at the direction her brazen thoughts had gone and she tried to look away. She couldn't. His dark, penetrating gaze nailed her in place, staring back at her in that way that always made her wonder if he could read her mind.

Charlee swallowed hard. She took in the length of his fit, muscular body and the way his massive biceps stretched the material of his gray polo shirt. Liam was powerfully built like an NFL wide receiver with broad shoulders that tapered down to a narrow waist, and long legs that took one step to her three. A big guy in a non-threatening way, but no less intimidating, he was the gentlest man she knew…until you got on his bad side. Then you were dead to him.

A stab of guilt pierced her chest as memories of the way their life together ended. If only she could have a redo. If only she could make a different choice where he was concerned. Then maybe the anxiety pulsing through her would subside. It didn't help that the intense, menacing silence that always pinged off of him surrounded her.

"Ahem."

Charlee startled when Kingslee cleared his throat. How long had she been standing there gawking at her ex?

She glanced at her dad as his hefty 6'2" frame moved past her and headed to the door.

"Liam, thank you for coming. It's good to see you again."

"You too, Mr. Kingslee," Liam said, referring to him the way most people around the city referred to him. Though he was shaking her father's hand, Liam's gaze slid back to her. "Charlee." His deep voice washed over her like warm honey.

Damn. She still had it bad for this man.

"Hi…Liam," she said around the lump in her throat. She needed to get out of there.

Beads of sweat peppered Charlee's hairline as she drew closer to him. It never failed. There it was again. Her body's visceral responses to him were mindboggling, each encounter eliciting a different reaction. Amped up heart rate. Sweaty palms. Nipples hardening. The list went on and on. There wasn't a thing she could do about it. Grin and bear it took on a whole new meaning during these moments.

Get it together, girl.

"Good seeing you again, Liam," Charlee murmured when she got closer to him, and then she glanced at her father. "Our conversation isn't over."

"Yeah, actually, it is. My mind is made up," he said gruffly. "Good luck with the meeting."

Charlee glared at the man who had raised her from the age of sixteen. She loved him to death, but there were times when he tested her beyond comprehension. Like now.

But that was okay. There'd been plenty of times when his "no" made her work harder to change his response to a "yes". She'd show him that she could have it all.

Even if it means finding a husband.

Chapter Two

Liam's heart and mind never led him wrong, except for where Charlee Fenlon was concerned. Part of him wanted to follow her out of the room and make sure she was all right, but the other part of him knew it was best to stay clear. She was still his weakness, and he was man enough to admit it.

But something was wrong. He saw it in her eyes. Felt it in his bones. Considering the tension in the room when he arrived, it was safe to assume that she and Kingslee weren't on the same page about something. But rarely did she let anyone get under her skin, not even him. Normally, those mesmerizing brown eyes held a bit of mischief, excitement, and usually her love for life could be felt upon meeting her.

Not today. Today she seemed down, and there was something else… Sadness. Frustration. Uncertainty. Three elements that weren't a part of her ardent personality.

He gave his head a slight shake. Her issues weren't his problem. *She* wasn't his problem. Only a fool would keep subjecting himself to the heartache Charlee tended to cause.

And I must be a fool. Because going after her was exactly what Liam wanted to do, but he stayed put. Whatever was going on, he planned to…

"I always wondered what happened between you and my daughter," Kingslee said, snapping Liam out of the trance that Charlee had unknowingly left him in.

Liam gave himself a mental head slap at being caught staring after Charlee. He didn't know how much Kingslee knew about their relationship, but he had no intention of sharing anything.

He had always been a private person, never wanting anyone in his business. Not even his nosey family knew about his short courtship with Charlee. Well, most of his family didn't know. His cousin, Jerry, found out over a year ago, but he hadn't shared Liam's big secret. That he was once engaged to be married to Charlee.

"A couple of years ago, shortly after you and Charlee met," Kingslee started as he sat at the head of the long conference table, "Charlee had mentioned going to dinner with you. Needless to say, I was pleased. The thought of her dating my mentor's grandson was more than I could hope for."

According to the stories Liam had heard, his grandfather, Steven Jenkins, and Kingslee had met during a meeting. A meeting that Kingslee had pulled together with several heads of construction companies in Cincinnati to discuss equipment needs. Since then, Kingslee and Liam's grandfather had been good friends and even golfing buddies.

"But whenever I questioned Charlee about the relationship," the old man continued, "she'd in so many words tell me to butt out." He chuckled, gesturing for Liam to take the seat in the chair to the right of him.

Liam pulled his laptop out of the bag and set it on the table before taking the seat that Kingslee pointed to. The last thing he wanted to discuss was Charlee, especially since he was there on business.

"At the time, she was happier than I had ever seen her, which was all I ever wanted. Then a few months later, something had changed. No matter how many times I tried to get her to talk about her personal life, she shut me out." He looked Liam in the eyes. "What happened between you two?"

Liam wondered why the guy was asking now. Jenkins & Sons Construction had done a couple of projects for him over the last few years, and Liam had seen him during some of those times. Not once did her father question him about Charlee. Why now?

"You'll have to ask your daughter," he said and glanced at his watch. "Nick should be up here shortly. Then we can get started." His cousin, the manager of Jenkins & Sons Construction, had met Liam there, but before they entered the building, Nick had gotten a call that he had to take.

After a slight hesitation, Kingslee said, "So it's like that, huh?"

Liam met his amused gaze. "Yes, sir." As far as he was concerned, conversations about Charlee or his personal life during a business meeting was off limits.

Kingslee nodded, looking thoughtful, tapping his pen against a pile of papers in front of him. "I like you, Liam. I'm not sure what, if anything happened between you two, but for the record, you're the type of man I'd pick for her."

Uhh...o—kay. What the hell am I supposed to say to that?

Should he tell her father that had things worked out as planned, he'd be married to his daughter and have at least one child by now? Or maybe he should tell him that no other woman had ever, and probably never will own his heart the way Charlee had. Or maybe he should explain to him that after the breakup, his heart had practically stopped beating because she was no longer in his life.

Liam didn't say any of that. He stared at the older man for a moment before dropping his gaze. He should be flattered by Kingslee's words, but after the breakup, he spent months trying to forget Charlee. When she resurfaced about a year ago, the anger festering since last seeing her came to the forefront. So caught off guard at the time, all Liam had been able to do was glare at her before walking away.

He could admit to being a world-class jerk. Since then, he was better around her but not much. Memories of how good they were together always got the best of him. Charlee had once owned his heart. She could've asked anything of him. He would've given it. But weeks after agreeing to be his wife, she had chosen her career over him and tossed his love back in his face.

Liam shook those thoughts free. This was not the time or the place to be daydreaming about his ex.

Minutes later, his cousin Nick entered the room. Not only was he a sheet metal worker by trade, but he was also the construction manager for Jenkins & Sons Construction. Their cousin, Peyton, had taken over the business after their grandfather retired, propelling it into a multi-million-dollar company before she married and moved to New York. Since then, Nick and some of their other cousins had turned it into the largest minority-owned construction company in the state of Ohio.

"Sorry I'm late, Mr. Kingslee," he said, shaking the older man's hand. "Good seeing you again."

"Same here, Nick. It's always a pleasure working with J & S. Thanks for being willing to meet me here."

"It's our pleasure."

Nick sat next to Liam and thankfully leaped right in. For the next hour, they discussed the renovations for the cottage Kingslee owned that was located just outside of Cincinnati. Liam had met him out there a few weeks ago to go over specifics, check out the layout, and make sure he had a good understanding of what Kingslee wanted.

"The wall of windows facing the stream is going to look amazing," Kingslee said, pointing at the rough drawing on the laptop screen. He asked a few questions about material, requested several changes, and Liam took notes.

He was done with his portion of the meeting but stuck around while Kingslee and Nick worked out a few other details. As the two men talked, Liam's mind drifted back to Charlee. From the moment they'd met, there had been

13

something about her that drew him to her like a magnet to steel. He hadn't planned on falling in love with her. They were as different as night and day.

He planned everything, while she was a fly by the seat of her pants type of person. He enjoyed cooking and quiet evenings at home, while she preferred to eat out and be around people. The louder, the better. Despite their differences, they clicked, balancing each other perfectly.

And then there was their lovemaking. Liam's body tightened just thinking about their sex life. They never had a problem in that area. There were times when he could still feel the weight of her firm breasts cradled in his hands or those long, toned legs wrapped around his waist. Hell, there were even times he could still taste her on…

"Liam?" Nick nudged him in the arm with his elbow, frowning as if asking, *What's up with you?* "Are you going to be able to deliver the final plans by the end of the month?"

Liam ran a shaky hand down his mustache and over his mouth not wanting to admit that he'd been half listening while fantasizing about Charlee. Rarely did he promise to complete plans in less than six weeks, especially since they were practically rebuilding the seventeen hundred square foot place. But the sooner he was done with this project, the better and the less chance he'd run into Charlee any time soon.

"I'll make sure they're done," he finally said.

Chapter Three

Charlee stumped up the three steps to her best friend's house, still fuming from the meeting with her father that morning. Despite how busy her day had been, thoughts of what he'd said about the CEO position kept seeping into her subconscious, making her angry all over again.

She stabbed her finger at the doorbell, impatience roaring through her as she stood on the threshold waiting for Rayne or Jerry to answer the door. Charlee hadn't called, but rarely did on a weekday and occasionally stopped by. She knew their routine. Jerry's work truck was in the driveway and right about now, Rayne would be cooking dinner for her family.

Charlee refrained from ringing the bell again, not wanting to chance waking Jay Jr in case he was asleep. But the moment Rayne opened the door, she stormed past her into the house. Charlee didn't have to look behind her to know her friend was staring a hole into her back.

"Hello to you, too. Come on in," Rayne said sarcastically, closing the heavy wooden door. "What's wrong with you? I don't think I've seen you this pissed since your father fixed you up with the owner of that pest control company."

Charlee grimaced at the memory. She would never allow her dad to set her up on a blind date again. Clearly, he had poor judgment and lousy taste in men when it came to her.

"What happened?" Rayne strolled toward the kitchen, Charlee following behind her.

"My father is what happened. The old man has finally gone too far," Charlee snapped, pounding her fist on the breakfast bar. "Ugh. Every time I think about our conversation from this morning, I get pissed all over again. Sometimes he makes me so angry. Do you know what he had the audacity to say to me?"

"No, but I'm sure you're going to tell me." Amusement flashed in Rayne's eyes.

It was nothing new that Charlee and her father bumped heads. Where he was patient, strait-laced, and focused, she was the opposite. Impatient. Non-planner. Charlee loved to bring fun into everything she did. It was a wonder she'd made it up the corporate ladder as quickly as she had, especially since she usually followed her gut when making decisions. Lucky for her it hadn't steered her wrong.

"He told me that even though I'm qualified, he wouldn't consider me for the CEO position when he retires."

Rayne's brows drew together. "Why not? I would think he'd want you to take over the family business."

"Yeah, you would think, but he was adamant about me not getting the position because..." The words dangled on the tip of her tongue like a bitter piece of fruit. "He's not promoting me to the position because I'm not married."

Rayne's mouth formed a perfect circle. "Whoa."

"I know right? What type of shit is that?"

"Language," Rayne reminded. "Stormy's upstairs. You know her hearing is sharper than that of a bat."

Rayne's daughter was the most precious little girl, and she was also Charlee's goddaughter. She loved that kid as if she were her own.

"Sorry, but I'm so disgusted with that man right now. It took all my restraint not to dive over the conference room table and strangle him today. I have worked my butt off to learn practically every aspect of that company since I was seventeen, and he has the nerve to say something like that to me."

"Did he give any other reason why he wouldn't consider you for the position? Surely that can't be the only reason." Rayne seasoned the chicken that she had in a pan before covering it with aluminum foil.

"He said that I was too much of a loose-cannon, untamed, wild, and unpredictable." He might not have said those exact words, but growing up, she'd heard them plenty of times.

She sighed. It didn't go unnoticed that her friend hadn't responded. Charlee could admit to being a risk taker, often following her gut to make major decisions, but her instincts were always on point.

"I never thought my own father could be a sexist, but he is," she mumbled absently. It hurt knowing that he didn't respect or appreciate the value she brought to the company. "Even if I was ready to get married, it's not like I can just pick up the phone and ask a man to marry me."

"Actually, you can. I know a guy."

Charlee spun around to find Jerry standing at the entrance between the kitchen and the stairs that led to the second floor. He was holding her three-month-old godson, Jerry Jr, in the crook of his arm like he would a football.

Jerry approached Rayne, looking at her like he always did, like she was a gourmet lollipop and he wanted to lick her all over. Charlee almost felt as if she should cover her eyes at the blatant way he undressed his wife with his eyes.

It was actually kind of sweet. Now at a size sixteen, Rayne had complained about not being able to lose the baby weight fast enough, but Jerry could care less. Back in the day, he had been known for being attracted to thick women and the way he was looking at his wife, it was safe to say that hadn't changed.

"Hey, beautiful," he crooned when he was in reach of Rayne.

She blushed, a small smile on her lips as her husband moved even closer and kissed her sweetly.

Charlee's heart melted a little bit each time she saw them together. She couldn't think of any other person more than Rayne who deserved the love of a good man. For much of her friend's life, she'd had one devastating blow after another...until Jerry came along.

"How was your nap?" she asked, caressing the light stubble on his cheek.

"It was good until this little guy woke up."

"There's my baby boy." Rayne kissed his chubby cheek and nuzzled his neck before returning her attention to Jerry. "It's awfully quiet upstairs. Did you look in on Stormy and Sunshine?" she asked of their six-year-old daughter and the puppy that followed her everywhere.

"Yeah, she's fine. She's on the phone talking to my mother."

"Oh, okay. Well, since Jay seems content at the moment, give him to Charlee. I want to cut up these potatoes before I feed him."

Charlee happily accepted the squirming little guy whose disposition was much like his parents. Rayne and Jerry were both pretty laid back, and junior was just as mellow. He rarely cried, and she had never seen a baby at his age who seemed so aware of everything around him.

Like now. He stared, gazing into her eyes as if searching her deepest thoughts.

"Hey, cutie-pie. How's my sweet boy?" Charlee's heart thudded against her chest when he flashed a toothless grin. He was definitely going to be a heartbreaker when he was older. His smooth dark skin and long eyelashes were like his father, but the light brown eyes were identical to Rayne's.

Jerry leaned his back against the kitchen bar and folded his arms across his chest, studying Charlee. Since marrying her best friend, he was the closest thing she had to a brother.

"Let's get back to your needing a husband."

"Let's not," she said quickly. "I don't know how much you heard, but I don't have a *husband* situation. Besides, I'm never getting married."

Charlee had missed her chance with the only man she would've ever considered marrying. She had no intention of opening her heart to another.

"Well, that's too bad, but if you change your mind in the next few minutes, you won't have to call anyone. Liam is on his way over. I have no doubt he'd help you with any situation." Jerry smirked and nudged her arm as he headed out the back door.

Charlee's pulse kicked up. Her first instinct was to leave before Liam arrived, but the other part of her wanted to see him again.

Considering Cincinnati wasn't all that big, it was a wonder they didn't bump into each other more often. After their breakup, many months had passed before she saw him again. As a matter of fact, the first time had been at Rayne's old townhouse, when she lived next door to Jerry. He and Liam had been hanging out, and Charlee happened to be leaving Rayne's place at the same time Liam walked out of Jerry's door.

To say the encounter was tense would be an understatement. If looks could kill, Charlee would've disintegrated into a heap of dust right on the spot.

Since Liam wasn't there yet, she still had time to leave before he arrived.

"Don't even think about running away," Rayne said as if reading her mind.

Charlee rolled her eyes.

"I know you might not believe this, but Jerry told me that Liam is still in love with you."

Charlee snorted as she rocked and swayed a little with Jerry Jr. who was drifting off to sleep.

"Liam stopped loving me the moment I put my career before him. Besides, that was almost two years ago. We both have changed, and I'm sure he's moved on." Charlee's heart ached. They would've been married had she chosen differently.

"I don't know why you're doubting his feelings for you. The heat between you two, whenever you're in the same space, crackles like hot timbers in a fireplace. Anyone in the vicinity can see the sparks. If that hadn't given it away, the way he looks at you speaks volumes."

"You mean the way he glares at me like I'm gum on the bottom of his shoe? Or are you talking about the way he makes himself scarce whenever I walk into a room?"

Rayne waved her off. "That's just a front, a way for him to protect himself."

"Yeah, call it what you want. I know better. He is so over me."

"I think he has tried to move on, but lately, I'm picking up a different vibe from him. There might've been a time when he was still angry, but Charlee I don't get that from him anymore. He wants you."

"Rayne don't go there. Do not turn into one of those people. Just because you and Jerry are crazy in love doesn't mean it's in the cards for the rest of us."

"I just want you to experience what I have with my husband. There is nothing like the love of a good man. Why can't you and Liam kiss and make up? Maybe you can make the first move and—"

"I've tried. He wants nothing to do with me."

"When did you try?"

"Shortly after we broke up. He's not the forgiving type, Rayne. I begged for him to give me another chance, promising never to put work before our relationship again."

"And what did he say?"

"He said I had already made my choice. Said that it was abundantly clear that my career meant everything to me. Then he told me to forget he ever proposed, and forget he even existed. Like that could ever happen."

20

Charlee would never forget him, his kisses, or the way her body still yearns for him.

She tried. On more than one occasion she tried to replace him, dating men who she thought could take her mind off of him. The only thing that accomplished was to make her realize what she had given up.

No. She would never love another the way she had loved...still loved Liam.

"I'm not putting myself out there like that again. So let's just drop it."

"Fine. Let's discuss your father instead. I've always been straight with you, Char, so don't take this the wrong way. But I agree *a little* with what he said about you being too impulsive."

"What? How can you say that?" she shouted.

The baby startled awake, and Charlee cursed under her breath. She started back rocking him until he drifted off again.

"I take my career very seriously and have never done anything that would jeopardize or embarrass the company."

"Here, let me take him. I'll lay him in the bassinet."

Charlee silently fumed as Rayne walked away, heading to the family room that could be seen easily from the kitchen.

How could her best friend side with her father?

"I've always been careful when it comes to the company," Charlee said when Rayne returned to the kitchen.

"I didn't say you weren't careful. I said you were impulsive. You're adventurous, and sometimes it spills into your professional life."

"There's nothing wrong with being adventurous. That's the problem with people, they're too uptight. It's okay to have fun sometimes, even in business."

"Like that time when you went skinny dipping on a dare in Brazil?"

"That was different," Charlee grumbled, hating that she had shared the story with Rayne. She had run into the guy at the beach, a distance away from the hotel that she'd been staying at. She had no idea that he was the buyer for the company that she was meeting with the next day.

"Or what about that time you danced on top of a bar during a birthday party, not knowing the birthday boy was someone Kingslee was in negotiations with? Your father was livid when he found out."

"Maybe he was, but he got over it *real* quick when it resulted in a six-figure sale. And why are you bringing up those instances? That was a long time ago. I'm not that person anymore." Charlee pouted, recalling a few other less than stellar moments over the years.

Maybe they were right about her being too impulsive, but she had never done anything reckless that reflected negatively on the company. At least not intentionally. What was most important was that the revenue she brought in and the processes that she had implemented had taken the company to the next level.

"You're supposed to be on my side," she said to Rayne.

"I am on your side. Always. How are you going to change your father's mind?"

Frustration lodged in Charlee's chest as she ran her fingers through her curly mane. "Why bother since he thinks I'm unfit to run the company."

Rayne swatted her arm. "Knock it off. You know good and well that's not the case. I bet he just wants you to have a life outside of work."

"Maybe." Charlee sighed, deciding her next steps. "I'm going to work my tail off and prove without a doubt that I'm the best person for the position. If that doesn't work, I'll have to go out and find some poor sap and beg him to marry me."

Chapter Four

Liam climbed out of his Chevy Camero, a little surprised to see Charlee's car parked in front of his cousin's house. What were the chances that they'd run into each other twice in one day? She was the last person he wanted to see. Not because she wasn't nice to look at. No, that definitely wasn't it. The problem was that each time he saw her, he couldn't get her out of his mind.

Had he not promised Jerry that he'd help with the addition to Stormy's swing set, Liam would climb back into his car and get as far away from there as possible.

But that would be a punk move, and he wasn't a punk.

His cell phone vibrated in his pocket just as he started up the front walk. He glanced at the screen and read the text from Jerry.

I'm in the backyard.

Instead of going through the front door, Liam redirected his steps. He walked around the side of the house and through the gate that put him in the backyard. Jerry was carrying a step ladder toward the swing set that was on the other side of the spacious yard.

"What's up, man?" Liam said.

Jerry turned to him, wiping his forehead with his arm. "Hey. I didn't know you were already here. I guess you got my text, huh?"

"Yep."

"I figured you might prefer a detour from going directly into the house since your woman is here."

Liam leveled him with a hard look, only making his cousin burst out laughing.

"She's not my woman. And keep it up, you're gonna mess around and not have any help out here."

He glanced at the large wood swing set that he and Jerry built for Stormy when they first moved into the home. Instead of buying a ready-made one, he and Jerry had customized the structure. It included a clubhouse-like fort up top with a window and pink awning, as well as a slide, acrobat bar, and a swing with room for two additional swings.

"Well, let's get to work. The sooner we get done, the sooner I can get your cranky ass away from my house."

For the next hour, Liam helped him add a baby seat to the swing set, but his mind was on the pretty redhead inside the house.

"You're quieter than usual. Does this have anything to do with Charlee being here?" Jerry asked, securing the last bolt that was holding up the swing. He climbed down off the step ladder and placed the wrench he'd been using back into the toolbox.

Liam said nothing. Seeing Charlee's fine ass twice in one day was too much. Fate was screwing with his peace of mind. Out of sight, out of mind had worked for him for a while, but now that she was back, he didn't know what to do with the warring feelings that lingered within him.

But if he were honest, he'd have to admit that each time he ran into his ex, the sight of her chipped away at the anger he had harbored toward her over the last couple of years. He was still pissed that she had chosen her career over him, but something inside of him had shifted.

"Do you remember when I first told you about the feelings I had for Rayne?" Jerry asked.

"Yeah, I remember."

They'd been at their cousin Nate's wedding reception. At first, Liam had thought Jerry was kidding. As a serial dater for as long as he could remember, Jerry loved women. Period. And he had vowed on more than one occasion he would never marry.

So when he confessed to being in love with a woman who wouldn't even go on a date with him, Liam hadn't taken him seriously. But months later, after pursuing her relentlessly, Jerry got the woman he claimed he couldn't live without as well as her cutie-pie daughter.

"That night, you said something about the Jenkins' men myth. How the men in our family know immediately when they have found *the one*. At first, I thought it was a load of shit," he said, but then grimaced and glanced around, probably looking for Stormy. He'd been trying to clean up his language since his daughter started repeating some of his bad words.

"I'm convinced that it's not a myth. It happened with me, Nick and Nate," he said of their twin cousins. "And my dad said it was the same with him and some of his brothers."

"Why are you bringing this up now? That was over a year ago."

"Just hear me out." Jerry took a swig of water from the bottle that had been leaning against the toolbox. "I've seen the way you look at Char—"

"Jay, don't start this mess."

Liam regretted ever telling him about his and Charlee's past relationship. It was a secret he had planned to take to his grave, especially since the situation made him look like a loser. And knowing Charlee hadn't shared the details of what went down between them with anyone, he had kept quiet.

But after Jerry married Charlee's best friend, causing them all to spend more time with each other, Liam had come clean with his cousin about everything, swearing him to secrecy. Despite them dating for a few months, and then being engaged for a few weeks, he'd had his reasons for keeping their relationship quiet.

Now, the last thing he wanted was for anyone in his family to know, especially his cousin Martina. She used juicy gossip about family members like dogs used chew toys, and she never let up until she humiliated them to no end.

"I know Charlee screwed up in the past, but you still have feelings for—"

"Uncle Liam!" Stormy screamed as she and her dog, Sunshine, bolted out of the house, the screen door slamming behind them. They ran towards them.

It always brought a smile to his face when she acted like she was happy to see him and added "uncle" to his name. Technically, they were now cousins, but shortly after her mother and Jerry married, Stormy started calling him Uncle Liam.

"What's up, squirt?" He tugged on one of her long ponytails that hung down her back and then kissed her cheek, eliciting a giggle from her.

It was impossible to be near the little sweetheart without smiling. She had an infectious grin, along with smooth brown skin, crazy-long eyelashes, and light-brown eyes that twinkled when she smiled, which was often.

"I have a new name," she announced, bouncing up and down on the balls of her feet as if she was on a trampoline and had ingested too much sugar. "Wanna know what my name is?"

Liam glanced at Jerry. He hadn't mentioned anything about a name change. His cousin's attention was on his step-daughter, the little girl he claimed as his own. Jerry had been smitten with Stormy from the moment he'd met her.

"What's your new name?" Liam asked. Her puppy, Sunshine, was sitting, staring up at Stormy, and Liam reached down and scratched the dog behind the ears.

"It's Stormy Violet Jenkins. I have my nana's name," she said of Jerry's mother and grinned harder.

She wrapped her little arms around Jerry's leg before he lifted her into his arms. He hugged her, peppering kisses on her face while she giggled and squirmed in his arms.

Jerry had started adoption procedures shortly after he and Rayne had gotten married. They thought the process would be simple since Stormy's biological father was deceased, but they ran into several delays.

"Is that right? You have your grandmother's name." Liam looked from her to Jerry, who looked like a proud father. "So it's official, huh?"

"It's official. Stormy is mine," Jerry said proudly.

"Daddy, can me and Sunshine get wet?" Stormy asked, giving Jerry that look that had wrapped him around her little finger early on.

Liam shook his head, smiling. His cousin didn't stand a chance against the kid's cuteness. God help him when she became a teenager. Actually, God help the little boys. Her future admirers wouldn't be able to get close to her. Jerry was fiercely protective of his wife, and that same behavior spilled over to his daughter.

He set Stormy on her feet. "Yeah, let me turn on the hose." He strolled across the yard with Stormy and her dog by his side. Liam watched as his cousin set up the kid-friendly water sprinkler on the other side of the yard. He barely got out the way before it started squirting water all over the area. Stormy and Sunshine ran through it. She was squealing with excitement, and her dog was barking with just as much enthusiasm.

"Now, getting back to what we were discussing," Jerry said when he returned. "When you gon' stop messing around with Abby...Autumn, or whatever your girl's name is?"

"It's Amber," Liam ground out, pissed that Jerry acted as if he didn't know the woman's name.

"Testy, testy are we? But anyway, seeing the way you be stealing glances at Charlee is all the proof I need to know that you're still in love with her. Which means, Amber is not the woman you truly want. What I don't understand is why you're wasting time with her when the one you really want is in my house hanging out with my woman?"

"Jay…it's complicated," Liam said under his breath, not wanting to discuss anything that included his ex. He bent down and started reorganizing the tools in the box in order to close it.

"I suggest you hurry and decide if you want Charlee back. Otherwise, it'll be too late."

Liam's hand froze on the lid, and he stood slowly. "What do you mean?"

"Your sister wants to set Charlee up with one of Zack's NFL friends."

Liam's sister, Jada Jenkins-Anderson, was married to a former NFL superstar. His brother-in-law had retired from football years ago but still kept in touch with many of his teammates. The last thing Liam wanted was for Charlee to hook up with some jock, but then again, she wasn't his anymore. She could do whatever she wanted. Yet, there was a part of him, the jealous-I-don't-want-anyone-else-near-her part of him, that didn't like the sound of this new development.

"Wait. Jada doesn't know Charlee, except for maybe seeing her once or twice here," he countered.

"She doesn't know her as your *ex-fiancée*, but thanks to my wife, they've met a few times outside of family gatherings. And Jada is trying to talk Charlee into being in her fashion show in a few months. I think Labor Day weekend or sometime around then."

With the help of a famous designer, his sister had recently started working on her own line of clothing. Liam knew about the fashion show, but he hadn't heard anything about her trying to recruit Charlee to be one of the models.

And a fine ass model she would be, he thought, as he rubbed the back of his neck.

"If JJ introduces her to some dude, you already know how that's going to go. One look at your woman and the guy is—"

"She's not my woman!"

"Oh, so you don't care if some chump pushes up on her? Man, she's a good-lookin' lady, and that's exactly what's going to happen."

As if conjuring her up, Charlee stepped out of the house and something too intense to identify flared through Liam's body. His heart jolted, and his pulse amped up at the sight of her.

Man, this woman. The effect she had on him was unnatural, like nothing he had ever experienced before...except for the very first time he'd seen her at Fenlon Manufacturing. Like then, he couldn't explain his reaction.

She continued standing near the back door, her long, auburn curls whipping around her face as the gentle breeze picked up. She pushed a few strands behind her ear and glanced around the yard. After tossing him and Jerry a quick glance, she directed her attention toward where Stormy and the puppy played.

But all Liam saw was Charlee.

His gaze slid from her hair to her face to her long graceful neck and slamming body. It was no wonder his sister wanted to feature her in the fashion show. The woman was gorgeous. She had the type of presence, the kind of exquisiteness that commanded attention. Any man with a pulse would take notice of her magnificence.

Her hands rested on her hips, causing the sheer, beige blouse to stretch over full breasts, sending all types of indecent thoughts through his mind.

His eyes went lower, taking in the tan slacks that hugged her slim, but shapely figure. On her feet were her customary high heels that she favored since she was only 5'5". Liam's gaze did a slow crawl back up her frame, and his heartbeat sped up as memories of her naked body sprawled out on his bed flashed through his mind. He knew the treasures hidden beneath the over-priced designer clothes and what he wouldn't give to see them again.

29

"Auntie Charlee, get wet with me," Stormy called out, bouncing around the sprinkler.

Charlee hesitated for a hot second, but then kicked off her shoes and ran toward her goddaughter.

Liam continued to watch. She was uninhibited, spontaneous, and an all-around good-time girl. She made a friend wherever she went and was the type of woman to leap first, then consider the consequences later.

Basically, she was everything he wasn't.

Playing in water, fully dressed, wasn't a big deal to her.

"See, that's the look." Jerry thumped Liam on the shoulder, effectively pulling him out of his trance. "She's the one you want, and there's nothing you can say to make me think otherwise."

At that moment, Charlee and Stormy started screaming and laughing uncontrollably, snagging Liam and Jerry's attention. Sunshine shook water off her fur, sending Charlee and Stormy into a fit of giggles as they moved away from the dog, who followed right behind them.

Liam couldn't take his gaze off of the woman. Soaking wet, water dripped from her hair as she pushed the tresses away from her face. His attention went lower, and his dick twitched, pressing hard and uncomfortably against the zipper of his pants. It was impossible to miss the way her nipples pebbled behind the thin blouse, sending more impure thoughts racing through his mind.

Damn this woman.

No matter how he tried to fight his attraction, she still had an effect on him. Hell, it wasn't just her hot body that made him yearn for her, but it was everything. He missed her. He missed what they once had, and it was getting harder and harder to deny.

"Go get Charlee a couple of towels," he said, barely sparing Jerry a glance.

"Okay, but not until you admit that you can't live without her," Jerry taunted.

"Jay...go get the damn towels!"

A burst of laughter trailed behind his cousin as he headed into the house. Sometimes the jerk was just as much of a pain in the butt as he used to be when they were kids, but Jerry was right about one thing. Liam needed to deal with his feelings for her.

But how?

Chapter Five

"Come here, Ladybug," Jerry said from near the back door, holding a towel for Stormy. She ran over with Sunshine right on her heels.

Charlee tugged on the front of her blouse, pulling it away from her wet skin before shaking it. What the heck had she been thinking, running into the water in her clothes, in her Chanel blouse at that? At least she'd had sense enough to kick off her shoes first.

Each time she moved her head, wet curls slapped back and forth over her face. Gripping the ends of her hair, she squeezed the long strands, forcing some of the water out as she moved toward the back door.

But her steps faltered.

Liam's long legs were carrying him across the lawn toward her, and Charlee's attention went to the light blue towels. A small one was tossed over one shoulder, while he carried a bigger one in his right hand.

From her peripheral vision, she noticed the moment Jerry ushered Stormy and the dog into the house, but Charlee's gaze stayed on Liam. The intense look in his eyes scorched every inch of her body. She recognized desire in a man's eyes when she saw it, especially if those eyes belonged to Liam Jenkins. It was a look she'd seen more times than she could count when they were a couple.

She was so vulnerable where he was concerned, but an unexpected thrill raced through her body. It had been forever since she'd been in his arms. Was it too much to hope that he planned to wrap the towel around her and hold her tight?

That's something he would've done at one time. A time when she didn't doubt his feelings for her. A time when he constantly professed his love for her. A time when she couldn't imagine her life with anyone else.

She shivered, then sneezed.

Oh no.

She sneezed two more times in succession.

Before realizing it, Liam was standing in front of her, holding the towel open and shaking his head.

"Come on so you can dry off."

Without hesitation, she stepped forward, anxious to get warm. Instead of facing him, Charlee turned and he slowly wrapped the thick cotton material around her trembling body. Carried away by the exhilaration of being near him again, she wasn't sure if he had pulled her closer or if she had bumped into him. All she knew was that a blast of heat shot up her spine as his arms encircled her.

Charlee searched her memory, trying to recall the last time they'd been this close. Trying to think of the last time a moment with him felt so intimate. Then she remembered.

She held back the whimper that inched up her throat as memories rushed to the surface. Hot. Steamy. Sex in the shower memories.

She missed what they once had. That thought was made even more prevalent while he held the towel tightly around her like he used to do after they showered. She treasured the moment and how good it felt to be in his arms again.

Liam lowered his head. His lips touched her skin, sending a tingle shooting through her body as he nuzzled the area behind her ear.

"Same ol' Charlee. Leap first and suffer the consequences later. You're going to have to get out of these wet clothes."

If only those words had a different meaning.

Her eyes drifted closed as he maintained his hold. The air was charged with a familiar feeling as he held her, and a sensual ache between her thighs blossomed.

The moment felt like a dream. Like one of her fantasies come to life, especially when he placed a feathery kiss against her neck.

Nope. This was definitely real.

His warm lips lingered, caressing as he nipped at her neck.

Charlee tried not to squirm, but no matter how hard she tried, she couldn't stop the moan that pierced the air.

Liam froze.

Considering how rigid his body suddenly went, it was as if he hadn't realized what he was doing.

She held her breath.

Didn't dare move.

Maybe if she remained perfectly still, he'd go back to what he was doing to her body.

No such luck.

As his arms loosened from around her, she wanted to beg him not to let go. Not to move away from her. But he slowly lowered his arms, and she fisted the towel in front of her.

She slowly turned and faced him.

Each time she was in his presence, he reminded her, without words, how much she missed him. His kisses, his hugs, heck, she even missed his world-famous lasagna. Basically, she longed for the man she should've been married to.

Sighing, Charlee lowered her gaze as a wave of guilt bombarded her. What would it take to get him to forgive her for throwing away their relationship? Was there a chance that Rayne was right? That Liam still loved her? Could he?

She lifted her eyes to his again. He still didn't say anything. He was the epitome of the strong, silent type. He wasn't a man who wasted words. He said whatever he meant, and when he didn't have anything to say, he kept quiet, no matter how much she would've preferred he talked.

Say something. Anything. Charlee silently begged.

A flare of heat sparked in his dark eyes and goosebumps trudged over her flesh, but when his gazed lowered to her lips no words were needed.

She knew what he was thinking.

She knew what he was remembering.

Them. Together.

Kiss me. The words blared inside of her head, hoping that he could somehow read her mind. Surely, he knew that she wouldn't push him away if he took such liberties. They were once so good together, like two metals perfectly molded into one.

Until they weren't.

A tickle started in her nose and she quickly turned her head and sneezed, then sneezed again, effectively breaking the spell.

As if suddenly remembering the other towel, Liam quickly snatched it from his shoulder and gently placed it over her head before stepping away from her again.

"Do you still keep a set of gym clothes in your car?" His voice was deeper than usual, encircling Charlee like a sensual embrace.

"Yes," she croaked out, then cleared her throat but sneezed again. "Yeah, I should probably go get them."

"Give me your keys. I'll grab them while you get out of those clothes."

Charlee nodded, too shocked to speak. She was super aware of him as he followed her into the house. Maybe this was a good sign. No. This was definitely a good sign.

Twenty minutes later, she had showered and changed in the guest bathroom before entering the kitchen. Everyone else had started eating.

"Help yourself. I'm sure you're hungry," Rayne said. She, Jerry and Stormy were sitting at the table, and Jerry Jr. was asleep in the baby swing nearby. Liam occupied one of the stools at the breakfast bar, his gaze steady on her.

Interestingly enough, his attention didn't unnerve her like it often did lately. Something had changed between them. She wasn't sure what, and didn't necessarily want to put a name to it. But being the opportunist that she was, Charlee had every intention of taking advantage of that development.

"Do you want anything else while I'm up? Another beer maybe?" she asked him quietly, wanting to do something, anything for him.

He shook his head. "I'm good."

After fixing her plate, she sat next to him and dug in.

God, this is good, Charlee thought, savoring every bite. She moaned with pleasure before she caught herself, hoping that no one heard her. Stealing a glance at Liam, it was safe to say she wasn't that lucky. His juicy lips twitched.

"I see you still enjoy your meals."

Charlee grimaced. "Uh, yeah. I guess some things haven't changed."

He nodded and a genuine smile spread across his mouth. A refreshing smile like a glass of lemonade on the hottest day of the year.

"I figured as much since you played in the water with your work clothes still on." He released a grunt, and before she knew it, his grin matched hers. "I always liked that about you."

At that moment, Charlee could've been knocked over with a feather. "Like what about me?" she asked, trying not to get too excited. Not only was he holding a conversation with her, but he was admitting to liking something about her.

"You. Living in the moment."

This wasn't the first time that he'd said that to her. He also used to tell her that she was everything he wasn't. That they were a prime example of opposites attract.

"Thanks for earlier...the towels," she explained, then sneezed into her arm.

Crap. She hoped she wasn't getting sick.

"You should probably take some vitamin C when you get home to ward off a cold."

Charlee nodded, trying not to get hopeful that he actually cared. Though she had apologized to him years ago for what she'd done to them, she felt an overwhelming need to apologize again. It was way past time they called a truce.

"Liam..." she started, her voice only loud enough for him to hear as she tried to figure out what to say. "I'm sor—"

"I'd better get going." He stood abruptly and glanced over his shoulder at those at the table. "I hate to eat and run, but I'm on deadline. Rayne, thanks for dinner. As usual, the meal was excellent."

"You're more than welcome," Rayne said when he carried his plate into the kitchen. "Oh, and just leave the dishes in the sink. I'll take care of them."

Feeling as if she'd just been punched in the gut, Charlee stared down at her plate as defeat crept through her body. Who was she kidding? There was no going back when it came to Liam. The sooner she embraced that fact, the better off she'd be.

Jerry stood, and he and Liam exchanged a man hug. "Thanks for your help with the swing. That should be the last addition for a while."

"Thanks, Uncle Liam," Stormy chimed from the table, her words sounding as if she was talking with her mouth full.

"No problem, princess. And Charlee..."

She glanced up, surprised to hear her name fall from his lips.

"Good seeing you again." With that, he and Jerry headed toward the front of the house.

"Well, that's progress," Rayne said as she strolled into the kitchen with empty plates. "At least he wasn't glaring at you this time."

"Yeah, there is that."

Charlee stuffed a fork full of green beans into her mouth. The emptiness she suddenly felt at Liam's departure made it clear that she wasn't over him. It didn't matter, though. Despite what Jerry said about her asking Liam to marry her, and Rayne claiming that he still loved her, there was no going back. Which was too bad. Charlee would give anything to get back with him, but she wasn't delusional. He would never give her a second chance.

Chapter Six

Liam trudged alongside Amber up the front walk that led to her small bungalow, dread weighing him down like a heavy quilt around his shoulders. Since picking her up an hour ago to take her to breakfast, he'd been trying to figure out how to get the inevitable conversation started.

"Oh, my goodness. I made a total pig of myself." She patted her flat stomach. "Deciding to have breakfast together was a good idea. It's been awhile."

"Yeah, it has." Liam slowed as they got closer to the house. He never wanted to do anything to hurt her, but he knew in a few minutes, that's exactly what would happen.

"You haven't said much since we left the restaurant. What's on your mind?" she asked over her bare shoulder and unlocked the front door.

Amber had that girl-next-door cuteness about her and was normally a more conservative dresser. But the red halter top she had on now was a little more risqué than her usual choice of clothing. He had noticed over the last couple of weeks that her wardrobe was slowly changing from business casual, to seductress chic. Not sure what brought on this side of her, but not even this new side of her could change what he was feeling these days.

He had to break up with her because Charlee still had a hold on his heart. At the moment, it sucked to be him, but he couldn't keep seeing Amber. It wouldn't be fair. There was no way he could be involved with one woman when his mind was always on another.

She's the one you want, and there's nothing you can say to make me think otherwise.

Jerry's words rattled around in Liam's head, taunting him as if his own thoughts of Charlee weren't already driving him crazy. It had been almost two weeks since the towel incident. Yet, a day hadn't gone by that he didn't remember how good she felt in his arms. How intense the pull was between them when he held her close. Or how he knew the moment he had stepped out of line. Having his arms wrapped around her lush body and inhaling her sweet scent had...

He had to stop this. He had to quit fantasizing about a woman who was no longer his. A woman who was his past. Which was where he intended to leave her.

"Liam?"

His gaze shot up only to collide with Amber's narrowed eyes.

"What's going on?" She set her purse on the table in the foyer before walking further into the house. "Are you feeling okay?"

"Yeah, I'm fine," Liam said a little too quickly then cursed himself for what he knew he had to do. He closed and turned the lock on the front door, and followed her into the living room. "But we need to talk."

His words stopped her. She turned slowly toward him, her back ramrod straight as if knowing something bad was coming.

Liam dropped his gaze and shoved his hands into the front pockets of his pants. He searched his mind for the right words to tell her that they couldn't continue seeing each other.

"Why don't we sit down," he finally said, gesturing toward the striped sofa.

She shook her head. "Whatever you're about the say, just say it."

"I can't see you anymore," he blurted.

Silence fell between them as she studied him, several emotions flashing across her face. Shock. Confusion. Hurt.

"Why?" she asked, taking a few steps toward him before stopping. "What…what happened?"

She was one of the nicest women he'd ever dated, but he had known for weeks, maybe even a month, that he didn't want forever with her. For the last six months, since they started dating, they got along great. They had a lot in common, laughed at the same jokes and connected on some levels. Liam had hoped that as they got to know each other better, his feelings for her would grow stronger. They hadn't.

Amber checked off many qualities of must haves on the life-mate list he had constructed in his mind, but there was still something missing. She didn't steal his breath away. She didn't make him lose sleep with thoughts of when they'd see each other again. And she didn't make him want to drop everything to be by her side.

That had only happened with one woman once in his life.

No matter how hard he searched or how hard he wished he could feel that…that…that *I-can't-live-without-you,* intensity again with someone new, it hadn't happened.

Not the way it did with Char…

Liam stopped the rest of that thought before it could fully form.

He stood in front of Amber and reached for her hand. "I'm sorry."

When a few tears leaked from her eyes, he pulled her into his arms. Placing a kiss against her temple, he held her, neither of them speaking for a few minutes.

"I can't believe you're breaking up with me."

"The last thing I want to do is hurt you but…"

She shoved gently against his chest and he dropped his arms to his sides.

41

"Then why? Why are you doing this? We're great together, Liam. I've done everything to become the person I thought you wanted me to be."

"Wait. What are you talking about? What type of person did you think I wanted you to be? I've never asked you to change, Amber. I like you. I like you just the way you are."

"Yet, you're breaking up with me."

"That's not because of you." He placed his hand on his chest and patted. "This is all on me."

She tsked and threw up her arms. "Oh, great. The it's not you, it's me speech. Don't give me that crap."

"Amb—"

"I'm so sick of this...this mess that guys like you dish out." She roamed around the living room aimlessly, her hands on her hips. "Each time I meet a nice guy, I'm all in, and he seems to really be into me, too. Only it usually turns out to be one-sided. God knows I hate dating. Just once I want..." She stopped and released a long, ragged sigh.

Liam didn't know what she was going to say, but when she didn't continue, he said, "I never meant to hurt you, Amber, but I don't know what else to tell you. This really is about me. I like you but...but I can't give you what I know you're looking for."

"And what would that be, Liam?" she bit out, more tears filling her eyes. "What do you *think* I'm looking for?"

He knew this conversation wouldn't be easy, but it wasn't going like he'd hoped it would. It would've been better if she'd just cursed him out, called him a few choice names, and slammed the door in his face. At least then he wouldn't feel like the lowest form of human life and have to see her cry.

"What? What do you think I want?" she bit out more forceful this time.

"Love," he said simply. "I know you're ready to fall in love, get married and start a family."

After a slight hesitation, she said, "And I thought we wanted the same thing. I thought we were on the same page, moving in the same direction toward the same goal." Now her words were pleading, only making him feel worse.

She was right. They'd had numerous conversations about the future, what they were looking for. They did want the same thing. He wasn't a fan of dating and had never like to date just to be dating. Rarely did he go into a relationship unless he thought it could lead to marriage.

"A few weeks ago, I told you that I loved you," Amber said, snatching a tissue from a nearby Kleenex box and dabbing at her eyes. "At least now I know why you didn't return the sentiment. Why didn't you just break up with me then? Why prolong…" She stopped moving and her back stiffened as she looked at him, really looked at him. "It's somebody else, isn't it? Have you been cheating on me?"

Liam's hands shot up and hurried to stop that line of questioning, shaking his head vigorously. "No. I wouldn't do that." A stab of guilt pierced him in the chest at how he'd held Charlee in his arms, wanting to do more than inhale her amazing scent and kiss her sweet neck. "But—"

"But you've thought about it."

The words were spoken so quietly, Liam barely heard them.

Amber folded her arms across her chest. "Why don't you tell me what's really going on."

He ran his hand over his head and let it slide to the back of his neck. He and Charlee weren't together and would never get back together. Yet, he couldn't get her out of his head. He couldn't get her out of his heart.

"There is someone else, but not the way you think," he rushed to say. "I was engaged almost two years ago."

Her eyes rounded. "Why didn't you ever tell me?"

He had never mentioned Charlee because he wanted to forget and move on from that time in his life. He also didn't tell her that he was embarrassed to admit that a woman who claimed to love him, had chosen a job over him.

"Liam?"

"Because it was my past. I had moved on." He strolled over to the brick fireplace where there were framed photos of her and her extended family. "Me and my ex were over long before you and I started dating."

"Is this why you never introduced me to your family, because you were still hung up on your ex?" she asked as if not hearing the part about him moving on. "Did you keep me hidden because you knew we weren't going to last?"

He didn't miss the bitterness behind her words, but he didn't respond. He hadn't introduced Charlee to his family either. Not because their relationship was a whirlwind that totally caught him off guard. No, that wasn't it. He never took either of them around the Jenkins clan because the last time he took his girlfriend to meet his family, it ended up being one of the most humiliating days of his life. Since then, Liam vowed that the next time his significant other met the Jenkins family, it would be at his wedding.

"So you're still in love with your ex," Amber said, snapping him back to the present. "Why is this coming up now?"

"Because I saw her recently and realized I still have feelings for her, even though she and I have moved on."

He didn't know what to do about Charlee. He couldn't go backwards, especially knowing that she would never have room in her life for him. When they were together, her career meant everything to her. He doubted that had changed, and he never wanted to risk coming in second again.

"I...I can't be with you while I'm still trying to work out my feelings for her," he explained. "You deserve better than that."

"Damn right, I do." Amber swiped at her tears and shook her head. "Only I would fall in love with someone who's in love with someone else," she choked out.

Regret crept through Liam. If he was honest with himself, deep down he knew he hadn't gotten over Charlee before he and Amber started dating. But he thought dating her would help him move on.

Amber blew out a noisy breath. "I think you should leave."

He approached her, but stopped short of touching her. "Not like this. Not when you're so up—"

"Please. Just go." She raised her teary-eyed gaze to his and the sadness he saw was like taking a punch in the gut. "I'll be fine." She headed to the door and opened it. "Have a good life, Liam."

Seconds ticked by while he stayed rooted in place. He didn't make it a habit of hurting women, and he wished that things could've turned out differently. He had hoped that she would understand.

Yeah, I'm an idiot.

What woman would understand him being with her while being in love with someone else? How the hell had he expected this conversation to turn out?

He walked out the door, but stopped and turn. "I really am sorry. I never meant..."

The door closed in his face. She hadn't slammed it, but closing it softly had the same effect.

Serves me right.

Chapter Seven

Liam preferred peace, order, and no drama in his life. Yet, his mind was a jumbled mess as he left Amber's place and drove to a construction site to meet with his cousin Martina.

The disappointment he'd seen on Amber's face had gutted him, made him wish that he hadn't gotten involved with her in the first place. In his mind, he knew that breaking up with her was for the best, but it still didn't make him feel any better about the situation.

I need a break from dating, he thought as he turned onto the land that his cousin Nate and their uncle Ben were developing. A few years ago, they had partnered and started a property development company, and now it was booming. This was their second major project, with another one in the works.

Liam parked and glanced around the sub-division that would eventually hold large single-family homes, as well as numerous townhouses. Construction had already started. Two of the model homes were complete, and the frame for the first row of townhouses was currently going up.

Stepping out of the car, he was immediately greeted by the chugging sound of heavy equipment, people yelling out instructions, and the smell of vehicle exhaust and dirt. He grabbed his hardhat from the trunk. He didn't venture out to job sites often, but always found it fascinating how so much went on and got done at the same time.

A loud whistle pierced the air and he turned. His cousin, Martina, stood outside of a model home, waving him over.

Liam headed in her direction, trudging over rocks and dirt and glad that he had thought to wear a pair of work boots.

"Thanks for coming, Cuz," Martina yelled over the drilling that was taking place nearby. "Let's go inside. It'll be a little quieter."

Liam followed her into the house, taking in the changes that had been made since the last time he was there. While she headed to the kitchen, he wanted to see how the rest of the home was staged. He stuck his head into a bedroom and then another before checking out a guest bathroom.

"Wow, the interior decorator did a good job," he said, strolling into the kitchen after his quick tour. Martina was standing near the center island where a set of blueprints was spread open.

"I agree. Everything is coming together nicely."

"So, what's up?"

"I figured it would be easier to show you some of the changes that Nate and Uncle Ben want versus trying to explain them over the phone."

Technically, Liam worked as an independent contractor, giving him the flexibility to set his own hours and come and go as he pleased. But he always made himself available whenever he was summoned by either Nick, Martina, or Nate. His attention went to the blueprint, the plans for one of the single-family homes. He had drawn them up over eight months ago.

Martina tapped a finger on the design. "You never cease to impress me with your skills."

Liam jerked his head up, shocked by her compliment. "Thank…you," he said slowly, bracing himself for an insult that was sure to follow.

Anyone who knew Martina Jenkins-Kendricks knew that she didn't dole out compliments often and any praise coming from her was huge. Insulting people was her thing, especially family members. Even though she and he got along more like brother and sister, he still wasn't exempt from her occasional needling.

"Yo ass ain't gotta act so surprise. You know you're good."

He chuckled. "Yeah, I know, but it ain't often that someone of your caliber says something nice about my work."

As the second in command at Jenkins & Sons Construction and a master carpenter, Martina was a perfectionist. It showed in everything she did, especially carpentry work. None of them could deny that she was the best at what she did and expected everyone else to be just as good. What she hated more than anything were slackers, and she didn't have a problem in calling any of them out.

She tsked. "I'm cool with giving compliments when they're deserved. It's just so rare that they're deserved."

She tugged on her baseball cap, part of her usual work uniform that went along with the J & S T-shirt, jeans, and steeled-toe boots.

"Anyway, Uncle Ben and Nate are thinking that they want to offer at least one home that doesn't have as much of an open floor plan. I was thinking the way the layout is on this one, it wouldn't take much tweaking."

"The city already approved these plans," Liam said, looking to see how much work it would take to add some walls and reconfigure this particular house. "Are they sure they want to go through that process again?"

"Yeah. They know it'll take at least a month to have them approved, but Uncle Ben said whatever it takes."

"All right, then. Tell me what you're thinking."

"I'd like to see," she started when her phone chirped, signaling a text message. She dug the device out of her back pocket. "That's, Gram. It still trips me out that she's texting now. Remember when she said that she would never respond to text messages? That if we wanted to talk to her, we'd better pick up a phone and call."

Liam smiled. Katherine Jenkins was the queen, and no one dared to defy her.

"Anyway, I'll call her back. Oh, before I forget, she was looking for you Sunday. She's starting to get a little ticked that you keep missing brunch. So what, you think you too good to hang out with the rest of us?"

Liam shrugged. "I was there a couple of weeks ago. Unlike the rest of y'all, I ain't tryin' to be there every week."

Sunday brunch was a big deal for the Jenkins family. Their grandmother insisted they all come together every Sunday afternoon and eat, hang out, and spend quality time together. Liam used to attend on a regular basis out of obligation, but for the last few months, he'd been limiting his visit.

He loved his family.

He enjoyed eating.

He even appreciated the camaraderie.

But he hated crowds.

They had always had a large, close-knit, boisterous family, but over the last few years, with all of the marriages and babies being born, the number of people seemed to have doubled. Despite the massive size of his grandparents' home, every week it felt smaller and smaller with all of the additional family members. But that wasn't his only reason for limiting his visits.

"If I didn't know any better, I'd think you were hiding something," Martina said as if reading his mind.

Liam shook his head. Sometimes this woman had the uncanny ability to see through the walls people constructed around themselves. She was what some would refer to as a busy-body, loud mouth, can't keep jack-shit to herself, pain in the butt family member. Normally, the two of them got along great, but Liam was a private person. He didn't go around sharing everyone else's business, and he sure as hell didn't go around blabbing about his own.

"I have nothing to hide," he said nonchalantly.

Martina folded her arms across her chest and leaned her hip against the counter. "Well, you better tell me what's going on with you. Otherwise, I'll just have to make something up. I haven't had any good gossip since I found out Sumeera, Liberty, and Toni were all pregnant at the same time. That's been almost a year ago now. I need some news. So speak up."

Liam shook his head. God, she got on his nerves, and he wasn't doing this with her today.

He returned his attention to the blueprint. "Instead of you trying to pry into my personal life, why don't we—"

"Hold up. Wait a minute." She stood upright and dropped her arms to her side. "Don't tell me this has something to do with that Sunday Royce showed up. Now that I think about it, you haven't really been around much since then."

Unease crawled down Liam's spine at the mention of his cousin. Leave it to Martina to notice everything.

She jammed her hands onto her hips, her mouth agape. "That's it, isn't it? That's why you never bring a woman around the family, and that's why you've been missing more Sundays than you've attended."

"Let it go, MJ," Liam warned.

Growing up, he'd been just as close to Royce as he'd been to his own brother, Adam. But one fateful Sunday afternoon had changed all of that. Royce had committed the ultimate betrayal, and he was the last person Liam wanted to discuss.

"You do realize that what he did happened like a hundred years ago, right? We were kids."

"We were grown." They had all been college age.

"Well, whatever. It was a lifetime ago. He lives like three or four hundred miles away, and besides a couple of months ago, he hasn't been to Sunday brunch in years. I think it's safe to say that—"

"Drop it, Martina," Liam said under his breath, trying to rein in the anger slowly inching its way to the surface.

Most people looking in from the outside thought the Jenkins clan was perfect. Thought the family didn't have some of the same issues as most families. Thought just because they were well-known and respected around the city, that drama didn't reside in their family.

It would blow their minds if they knew the truth. Betrayal. Extra-marital affairs. Yeah, if they knew half of what went on in his family, they'd definitely look at the Jenkins clan differently.

This particular incident that his cousin felt she just had to bring up was a moment in Liam's life that he'd rather forget. Finding your cousin in a bedroom screwing your girlfriend had a way of changing you. Unfortunately, when Liam caught them in the compromising position, Martina had been with him. It was because of her that he hadn't killed Royce.

But out of all that had happened back then, what surprised him the most was that Martina hadn't mentioned the incident. Not to him or anyone, which was shocking. Normally, no secret was safe with her, but she never said a word. Until now.

"I can't believe you're—"

Liam pounded his fist on the counter and glared at his cousin. "Martina, so help me... If you don't shut the hell up, I will strangle you," he said through clenched teeth. Some days, talking to her was like talking to a concrete slab.

"Fine! Geesh, you don't have to get your shorts all twisted. I was just making conversation, but for the record, let that mess with Royce go. That girl isn't worth it, and I'm sure Royce hasn't lost any sleep over it and has probably gone on to steal someone else's girlfriend. You..."

"Dammit, MJ! We either discuss the changes Uncle Ben and Nate want, or I'm out of here."

She huffed out a breath. "Okay, I'll drop it, but this ain't over. We will discuss this again. *Now* let me tell you the changes *I* want done to this plan."

*

An hour later, Liam left the construction site, more than ready to get away from Martina. She had a knack for getting under his skin. Of course, she hadn't dropped the topic of Royce. She might've been trying to be encouraging by telling him he needed to forget about that situation, but all that did was remind him of Royce's betrayal.

He had never been good at forgiving or forgetting. The only reason he didn't often think about his cousin was because Royce and his brothers had relocated to Chicago years ago. As far as he was concerned, Royce could fall over a cliff and he wouldn't go looking for him.

Liam drove in the direction of his favorite coffee shop. A few minutes later, he pulled into the small parking lot. Once he was out of the car, the sun's merciless heat bore down on him and beads of sweat graced his forehead. The average temperature in Cincinnati that time of year was eighty-two, but at the moment, it felt more like a hundred degrees.

Anxious to get into the air-conditioned building, he hurried across the lot, but slowed when he rounded the corner of the building. He almost bumped into the homeless man sitting a few feet from the entrance.

Despite the heat, the guy wore a dirty, gray hoodie laden with dark sweat stains, along with dark jeans and winter boots. How could someone stand to sit in the hot sun, covered with winter clothing and not pass out? Just as the thought crossed his mind, a slight breeze in the air carried the stench of sweat and mustiness past Liam's nose.

Holding his breath, he quickly dug into the front pocket of his pants for his money clip and removed a few bills. Life was tough enough when you had a job. He couldn't imagine how hard it must've been living on the streets, trying to hold onto hope that things would one day turn around.

He dropped a five, and five singles, into the beat-up hat that the man held with filthy hands.

"God bless you," the guy said, making eye contact before quickly looking away.

Seconds later, Liam entered the building. The smell of freshly brewed coffee and sweet treats with a hint of cinnamon greeted him at the door. Baristas calling out orders and the hum of several conversations, laughter, and dishes clattering, filled the air. This was the perfect distraction for what ailed him. For a Saturday afternoon, there were more people than he expected. The mom and pop shop was popular in the neighborhood, still hanging on despite a Starbucks moving in a few blocks away.

"Well, if it isn't one of my favorite Jenkinses," Anabelle said, smiling when he finally reached the counter.

The laugh lines around her eyes and mouth were the only giveaway that she was pushing seventy. Otherwise, she didn't look a day over forty. She and her husband, Sam, had been a fixture in the neighborhood for as long as he could remember.

"Hey, Mrs. Anabelle. How's it going?" Liam asked.

"A little busy, but I'm doing all right for an old lady. How's the family? I haven't seen your grandpa in here lately."

"Everyone is doing well, and you know Pops. He's always busy with some type of work even though he's supposed to be retired."

They talked for a few minutes longer before Anabelle took his order and he stepped to the side. While he waited, Liam glanced around, hoping to spot an empty table but didn't see anything. It wasn't until he had his coffee and cream cheese danish did he notice a man and a woman sliding out of a small booth on the other side of the room.

Skirting around the lines and a group of teenagers heading to the door, Liam was careful not to jostle the hot liquid in his hand. He made it to the table before anyone else could snatch it up. Once he was settled, he took a careful sip of the steaming, hot liquid and sighed. It didn't matter that it was eighty degrees outside, he rarely went a day without a hot cup of coffee and that one made number three.

Pulling out his cell phone, he scrolled through news articles displaying on his screen. He stopped at the one about a popular rapper and the latest trouble he'd gotten into. Part way through the article, the hairs on the back of Liam's neck stood and a sensation he hadn't felt in weeks raked over his skin. The air shifted. He knew without looking up who had just walked into the building.

He lifted his gaze and sat back in his seat as his heart rate sped up at the sight of Charlee. She strutted into the coffee shop looking like every man's fantasy woman.

Liam didn't know where she'd been or where she was going, but the white, fitted halter dress that stopped just above her knees was definitely a show stopper. It highlighted all of her assets.

She was already a stunning woman. But the way her usual wild curls were piled on top of her head and the way the dress hugged her lush body, only highlighted just how gorgeous she really was.

If the attention she was garnering was any indication, he wasn't alone in his assessment. Then again, it might not have been just the sight of her that grabbed other's attention.

She wasn't alone.

With a hand on his back, Charlee guided the man she was with toward the counter. It was the same homeless guy who'd been sitting in front of the building. What Liam didn't understand was why he was with Charlee.

He couldn't hear what she was saying to him, but the man lifted his hand and shook his head as if to say no, that's okay. But Charlee being Charlee, wasn't taking no for an answer. While she ordered, the guy headed toward the restrooms.

And Liam watched the woman he couldn't stop thinking about.

He watched, taking in all of her beauty.

He watched because he couldn't take his gaze off of her.

Once their order was placed, she and the nameless man headed to a small, round table not too far from the entrance. Both seemed oblivious of the attention they were garnering. Some patrons even moved away from them.

Liam shouldn't be surprised by Charlee's kindness. He had seen the time when she had taken off her coat, in the dead of winter, and gave it to a homeless woman on the street. Then there were the times when she'd dig around her purse for spare change to give to someone in need. Next to his mother and grandmother, she was the kindest and most generous person he had ever met.

Clearly, that was something else about her that hadn't changed.

When the barista called her name, Charlee hurried to the counter and returned to the table with two carry-out cups and a white paper bag. She kept one cup, probably a caramel macchiato, and set the other one in front of the man along with the paper bag. She nodded toward the items, encouraging the guy to indulge.

They sat together with her doing most of the talking as if the man was an old friend. Liam tried to ignore the smoldering desire that engulfed him whenever she was nearby. It was no use. Since the day in Jerry's back yard, memories of passionate nights and hot sex with her occupied his mind. But it wasn't just about how good they were together in bed. No, it was everything about the woman and the way she made him feel.

"I'm doomed," he muttered under his breath and lowered his gaze to his phone. He needed to regain some control. He couldn't keep carrying on like some love-sick puppy.

Clearly, that was going to be easier said than done. Every nerve in his body was attuned to her as he observed Charlee with the homeless guy.

Maybe they knew each other. This wasn't their first encounter if how close the guy was sitting to her was any indication. Like her usual, overly friendly and trusting self,

Charlee didn't seem to notice or care. She listened intently, smiling throughout the conversation. Liam didn't like the way the guy kept touching her. He'd seen first-hand how filthy his hands were. Who knew where the guy had been, or what he'd done out on the streets?

Charlee's smile slipped, and Liam straightened. She was uncomfortable. The way she leaned away slightly as they continued talking spoke volumes. Uneasiness showed on her face, especially when the guy touched her arm.

A possessiveness Liam hadn't felt in a long time fizzed inside of him.

Do not go over there.

She is none of your business.

What she does is none of your business.

Do. Not. Go. Over. There.

Chapter Eight

Charlee hated seeing anyone living on the streets, especially Everett. This was her third time running into him in the last eight months, but she thought the last time he'd been on the street would've been the last time. She had found him a job. Yet, here he was.

The guy was smart, funny, and probably a really good-looking man at some point. But a year ago he lost his job, his wife left him, and he couldn't seem to catch a break. When she first ran into him, he'd been off and on living in a shelter, and only able to get daywork on occasion. He made her believe that he wanted to work, but maybe she'd been wrong.

And maybe inviting him in for a cup of coffee and something to eat might not have been the best idea. He was getting a little too…handsy.

"Everett, why are you back on the streets?" Charlee finally asked. "What happened to the building maintenance job? I thought the position was yours."

He gave a slight shrug. "It didn't work out."

"Why not?"

"I didn't have a permanent address when I filled out the application. So I gave them the one to the shelter. They made me think that the job was mine, but then they did a background check. Everything was fine until I couldn't verify my address, and they claimed I lied on the application. At the time I applied for the job, I was staying there, but then I wasn't anymore and…anyway, it didn't work out."

Charlee shook her head. So much for trying to help. When she gave him the information about the job, she hadn't considered logistics. Apparently, going from homeless to employment wasn't as easy as she thought.

"I'm so sorry that job didn't work out, but you can't give up, and you can't keep living on the street. You need to keep looking."

She wished she could think of a way to help him. Based on earlier conversations, he had too much potential to be wasting it hanging out on the streets.

"Once I get enough money, I'll get a mailbox at UPS. That'll give me a physical address that I can put on applications."

"That's a great idea." Charlee grabbed her handbag. "How much do you…"

He stopped her, covering her hand with his. "No. I told you before. I'm not taking your money. I appreciate you, but you've done enough."

Charlee eyed the hand that was covering hers. She swallowed, trying to push down the bile crawling up her throat. She never wanted to come across as the type of person who thought they were better than someone else, but his touch made her skin crawl. That and his dirty fingernails had her wanting to snatch her hand away and leap into the nearest shower.

And God help her. He smelled awful. What had she been thinking, inviting him into the place where others were eating?

"A few weeks ago, I was able to do a little work for that lawn service guy you introduced me to. He only needed me for a few hours, but I made enough to buy me a few meals. So thank you for that."

He squeezed her hand and leaned a little too close, forcing Charlee to lean away from him. He seemed oblivious of his horrid scent and lack of hygiene. Her gag reflex was nearing its limit. Instead of asking him to move his hand, she eased out of his hold and sat her bag in the chair next to her.

"So what would your dream job look like?" she asked. She almost wiped her hands down the side of her dress until she remembered she was wearing white. There wasn't any lingering dirt, but the fact that he'd put his hands on hers kind of wigged her out.

"Right now, all I want is a job. It doesn't have to be a dream job. Just something to get me back on my feet."

Charlee nodded her understanding, wondering if the director's position was her dream job. She should've asked herself that question a long time ago before investing so many years into learning the business. The conversation with her father weeks ago still plagued her mind. His accusations of her not having a life outside of work bugged the heck out of her, and sadly, she didn't know how to do anything but work.

"Are you doing okay? You look tired," Everett said, a frown creasing his forehead.

"Oh yeah, I'm fine. Just putting in a lot of hours."

She was actually beyond tired. Her eyes had popped opened at six o'clock that morning, on a Saturday, and she'd been in the office by seven. There never seemed to be enough hours to finish everything. Now the days and even longer weeks were running into each other and at times Charlee didn't know if she was coming or going.

But determination drove her. That CEO position would one day be hers. Unfortunately, she wasn't the only person vying for the job. Bradley Handler, Director of Manufacturing, who happened to be her father's protégé and actually a nice guy, was working just as hard.

"I thought you were the boss," Everett said, interrupting her thoughts. "Shouldn't you be able to delegate some of whatever has you stressed out?"

If Charlee didn't know any better, she'd think Everett had been talking to her father. "I'm not stressed, it's just..." She didn't bother finishing the statement. In all honesty, she was a little tense, but it wasn't just about work. It was everything. Her father made her realize that her life hadn't unfolded the way she had envisioned.

Charlee sighed and took a careful sip of her caramel macchiato, savoring the sweetness on her tongue. It was her go-to coffee product, but maybe she should've opted for a shot of espresso instead. Anything to give her more energy to get through the rest of her busy day. She had an early evening dinner party to attend, as well as a birthday celebration later that night. Yet, what she really desired was a nap.

"Even stressed, you're still the prettiest woman I've had the pleasure of spending time with lately," Everett said, the compliment coming out of nowhere. He stretched his arm across the back of her chair. "Maybe once I get back on my feet, you'll let me take you out."

Charlee eyed him, a smile playing around her mouth. Amused that he was flirting with her even though he was homeless. If only he could use that charm toward getting a job and pulling his life back together.

"We'll see," she said, knowing she had no intentions of ever going out with him. He was intelligent and a nice guy, but she could already tell that he didn't have the type of drive and determination she looked for in a man.

"Oh, I almost forgot. I have a pay-as-you-go phone." He patted the pocket of his sweatshirt. "Let's exchange numbers before you leave," he said, then surprised the heck out of her when he started massaging her shoulder.

"Um," Charlee leaned forward, trying to wiggle out of his hold without letting on just how grossed out she was. "Ev—Everette, I don't—"

"Get your hands off of her."

Charlee startled. The low, lethal demand came from behind her, and she glanced over her shoulder. Her breath stalled in her chest at the sight of Liam, looking sexy as usual with a baseball cap pulled low over eyes that were glaring at Everette.

Where had he come from?

"I said—Get. Your. Hands. Off. Of. Her."

"And who are you supposed to be?" Everette frowned, but sat up straighter. "Wait, you're the guy who gave me money a few minutes ago. So what? You think just because you toss me some change, I have to do what you say?"

Charlee shook his hand free of her shoulder, but then it slid to her back.

Amused, the corners of Everett's lips quirked as he kept his attention on Liam. "What she and I do is none of your business. Besides—"

"She *is* my business. Now move your damn arm or lose a hand. Your choice."

Charlee's mouth dropped open. The short while that they'd dated before getting engaged, she had witnessed Liam's possessive side. It never made her uncomfortable and he was never rude to anyone. In fact, she actually loved the attention, but right now, he was way out of line.

She started to tell him that but thought better of it. Deciding to give him a piece of her mind when Everett wasn't around.

"Come on. Let's go," Liam said, boldly inserting himself between her and Everett.

But Everett wasn't having that. "Now you wait just a—"

"Actually, Everett, I really should be going." Charlee stood abruptly, noting they were garnering attention. There was no need to let the conversation get even more out of hand. "It was good seeing you again. Take care of yourself."

"Charlee, you don't have to—"

"Yeah, actually, she does."

Without another word, Charlee maintained her cool and let Liam guide her toward the exit, his hand resting at the small of her back. Despite being pissed at him, her skin tingled at the electric currents charging through her body, not surprised that his intimately familiar touch had the opposite effect as Everett's.

The smart part of her brain was telling her to move away from him since she was struggling to ignore the heat from his fingers and the way it seared her body. But that other part of her, the part that had missed him more than she thought, wanted his large hand to move lower, and then even lower than that, which was crazy.

He had just embarrassed her, treated her like some kind of property, and was walking her out of the building like he was her man.

"Liam," she said, starting to turn to him before they reached the door. He needed to know that just because she was walking out with him, didn't mean that he could butt into her business whenever he felt like it.

"We'll talk outside," he mumbled gruffly under his breath. He slipped on his dark shades and now kept her moving with a gentle hold on her elbow.

Charlee practically stomped toward the parking lot where she'd left her car. At the moment, it didn't matter that she was probably behaving like a brat. Lips poked out, eyes shooting daggers, while she mumbled under her breath. The last couple of encounters with this man was driving her insane. Some of his actions made it seem as if he had forgiven her and was ready to call a truce. But other times, like right now, she wasn't sure what to think.

"I cannot believe you just did that," she fumed, only loud enough for him to hear. They sidestepped a few people on the sidewalk. Some heading into the coffee shop, while others walked in the opposite direction.

Charlee already knew Liam wouldn't respond until it was just the two of them. Normally, he wasn't confrontational and for the most part, a very quiet and private person. She didn't know what had gotten into him back there.

Maybe befriending Everett and spending those few minutes with him hadn't been the smartest or safest thing to do, but she never sensed any danger from him. It wasn't a crime to do something nice for someone, like buy them coffee.

In all honesty, she understood Liam's frustration. She had gotten herself into some jams in the past and neglected her safety a time or two. According to him, she was too trusting. But she couldn't help it if she didn't roam around expecting the worst of people. That's not how she operated. She treated people, no matter who they were, how she wanted to be treated until they did something to betray her trust.

The short walk to the parking lot was doing Charlee good as her anger slowly dissipated. She wasn't sure where Liam was parked, but he followed alongside of her, neither saying anything as she headed to her white Lexus. It wasn't until she unlocked the door and tossed her purse inside that she whirled around on him.

"What the heck was that back there? What were you thinking, acting as if you care anything about me!" she shouted.

Okay, so maybe she was still a little ticked off, but he had some nerve.

Liam got in her space, close enough for her to smell the alluring scent of his cologne. Though he was crowding her, tempting her to launch into his arms and cover his full, kissable lips with hers, Charlee stayed put. She couldn't see his eyes behind the dark aviator shades, but no doubt he was glaring down at her.

"Why do you always put yourself in dangerous situations?" His voice was calm, but she heard the edge in his tone. His barely controlled anger was peeking out.

"Liam, how was that dangerous? I've seen him here before and I know Everett. He wouldn't hurt me. I was doing something nice for someone who was down on his luck. That's all."

Liam snatched off his sunglasses and leveled her with a hard glare. "By letting him put his frickin' hands on you?" he snarled. "Come on, baby. You're smarter than that. The guy is living on the street. God knows where he or his hands have been. Yet, I look across the coffee shop and find him caressing you!" His voice grew louder with each word before he caught himself. He cursed under his breath, noisily exhaled, and took a small step back.

Yeah, Everett had weirded her out a little, but Charlee knew he didn't mean to make her uncomfortable. But Liam was right. Just because she and Everett were always friendly, didn't mean that it was a good idea to get too close.

She sighed and stared down at her strappy, white sandals. Of all the people to run into, why'd it have to be Liam? It had already taken her awhile to finally stop thinking about him every minute of the day. Now that he was standing there— still close enough to touch—he had ruined her peace of mind. She'd probably be thinking about him for the rest of the day.

"You're too trusting," he said with more calm. "When are you going to learn that you can't save the world?"

"I'm not trying to save the world," she grumbled. "All I try to do is spread kindness wherever and whenever I can."

Okay, that might've sounded like some type of proverb, but it was true. If more people extended a kind gesture, maybe the world wouldn't be so screwed up.

"Oh, please. Stop trying to justify—"

"Fine! Sue me if you have a problem with that, but what I don't understand is why you have a problem with anything I do? It's not like we're together anymore. Normally, you can't stand the sight of me. Looking at me sometimes like I have shit on my face. So what changed? Why do you care now, Liam?"

Silence so thick, it could be cut with a chainsaw fell between them. The expression on his face gave nothing away. If he wasn't staring so hard, she wouldn't have been sure that he'd even heard her.

"I care," he finally said, shocking the heck out of her. Her heart flipped over at the revelation. "And I don't like to see other men's hands on you. Stay the hell away from that guy."

Charlee stood dumbfounded, unable to put an intelligent sentence together as he slipped the sunglasses back in place. He started to walk away but stopped. With one hand on the opened car door, he gestured toward the driver's seat.

"Get in. I'm not leaving until you do."

As her mind reeled, Charlee clumsily climbed into the vehicle on autopilot while he held the door. She might not be able to actually see his eyes with the dark shades, but she felt him staring. As usual, she wasn't sure what to make of him. The man was such an enigma, always managing to throw her off balance.

He didn't close the door until she stuck the key in the ignition and started the car, then he walked away. Charlee knew him well enough to know that he was probably parked somewhere that he could easily see when she left. But she sat there in stunned silence, her body still vibrating from being in such close proximity to Liam. Her heart and soul were so intricately consumed by him.

Will I ever really be able to move on with my life without him?

Until recently, Charlee thought she had. Apparently, she hadn't.

She quickly used the hand sanitizer that was kept in the car. While she rubbed her hands together, she glanced in the rearview mirror. Liam's relaxed gait carried him across the parking lot to the last row.

Even as she drove out of the lot and on to her next destination, Charlee couldn't wrap her brain around what had just happened. Her frustration about what took place in the coffee shop had fled her mind. It was Liam's admission that rocked her.

I care.

Those two simple words that he had spoken held more promise than anything he had said to her over the past year. How many times had she tried to make amends? Or begged God to work it to where she got a second chance with him? Off and on since they'd gone their separate ways, she wanted to believe that a reconciliation was possible. After today, after witnessing his strange behavior and the admission that he still cared, she was more hopeful than ever.

Maybe her prayers were finally being answered.

Chapter Nine

Liam banged his fist on the steering wheel. "I have lost my mind!"

What had he been thinking getting into that guy's face? Hell, he hadn't been thinking. Yeah, he was pissed about seeing the asshole's hands on Charlee, but it was none of his business. *She* was none of his business. Despite him telling the homeless guy otherwise, Charlee wasn't his concern. She was a grown woman, capable of taking care of herself just fine without him.

Then why was he tripping? Why was he still so riled up, ready to go back to the coffee shop and pummel the guy?

Because the woman makes me crazy...still.

Shaking his head, Liam started the car and revved up the engine before peeling out of the parking lot. He needed to get a grip, but damn if he couldn't stop thinking about Charlee.

A walking, talking temptation.

When she got into her car, and the hem of the too tight, too short, too sexy, white dress slid up her shapely, toned thighs, he almost lost it. It had taken every bit of willpower he possessed not to pull her to him and ravish her body and taste her sweet lips again.

That woman is going to be the death of me.

It was as if God was playing some cruel trick on him, messing with his emotions and making him behave like an idiot.

Charlee is not mine. She does not belong to me.

The words played on a loop over and over inside his head but weren't helping. He wanted her. God help him. He still wanted her.

He pressed the volume button on the steering wheel of his Chevy Camaro in an effort to drown out thoughts of Charlee. She had spent enough time in his head over the past couple of years. And just when he thought he had moved on, she showed back up in his life.

What were the chances that they'd keep running into each other? What were the chances that his cousin would fall for her best friend? That made it almost inevitable that they'd see each other from time to time, but why'd he have to see her today?

"I'm doomed."

Liam almost laughed out loud when Michael Bolton's raspy voice blared through the car speakers as he crooned *When a Man Loves a Woman*. The lyrics resonated with him. There had never been a more perfect song to describe his feelings for Charlee, and that scared him to death. Even after she chose her job over him, his love for her hadn't died.

How is that possible?

How could he still love a woman who hadn't felt the same for him back then? Yet, lately, he'd been longing for her like he used to when they dated. When she'd travel for work, be gone for weeks at a time, there were days he thought he'd lose his mind. On occasion, he'd fly out to be wherever she was in the country, only to miss her that much more when he returned home.

"I can't put myself through that again," he mumbled to himself.

Succumbing to the fierce attraction that still lingered between them, or getting even more emotionally involved with anything concerning her was asking for trouble.

*

Liam stood slowly from his leather sectional and stretched his arms high above his head. He'd been sitting for the last couple of hours watching a baseball game on TV.

"Now *that* was a good game." He yawned, his tired body starting to feel the effects of the long day.

"I agree, but the Yankees were cutting it close. Boston made them work for that one." Jerry stood as well, twisting and turning to stretch out his back.

"I know, right? I'm just glad it didn't go into extra innings. I need to get home." Nate carried his empty plate, beer bottle, and used napkins to the kitchen. His brother Nick following suit.

"Thanks for letting us crash over here," Nick said, rinsing the plates and loading them into the dishwasher.

Liam chuckled. "Like I had much of a choice."

Nick had called a few minutes before the game started, saying he was on his way over. A few minutes later, Liam was letting him into the house, along with Nate and Jerry who strolled in behind him carrying chips and beer.

"You had a choice, but we probably would've shown up anyway," Jerry added, storing what was left of the bag of potato chips in the pantry along with a container of homemade cookies that he'd brought with him.

Liam accepted a plate from Nick and put it in the dishwasher. "I see your wives have taught you guys well."

They all pitched in tidying up the kitchen and the living room where they'd been camped out in for the last few hours.

"Our wives should probably be thanking Gram and Sunday brunch," Nick grumbled, and the rest of them joined in. There'd been a time when the women in the family cooked and cleaned on those days. That had changed. Their grandmother had enacted a schedule that included all of them taking turns being on clean-up duty.

"By the way, the lasagna was almost as good as mine." Jerry wrapped up what was left of the dish and placed it in the refrigerator.

"Whatever. None of y'all can hold a candle to my lasagna so don't even try and front." Lucky for them, Liam had fixed dinner before knowing that he would be having company.

Most of the men in the family enjoyed cooking and had been taught at a young age. Though his mother was a good cook, it was his father who had taught him. Liam still remembered the cooking lessons. It started with him learning how to prepare breakfast items when he was around five years old, and gradually Lee Jenkins had taught him enough to where Liam could cook full meals. To this day, his father was still the main cook in their immediate family.

Nate glanced at his watch. "Man, I didn't realize it was this late."

"I'm surprised Liberty hasn't called you to come help with the twins," Liam said, strolling into the living room. No matter where he stood on the main level of the house, the open floor plan gave him an unobstructed view of the living room, dining room, and the kitchen.

"Liberty's sister is spending the weekend with us. Otherwise, I'm sure she probably would've called a couple of hours ago."

Liam marveled at how much the family dynamics for his cousins had changed in the past year. Nate and Liberty had six-month-old identical twin boys who were born three months after Nick's youngest daughter. Add in Jerry's baby boy and they were well on their way to building a co-ed basketball team.

"Man, Liam, you're the last hold-out. When are you going to take the plunge?" Nick asked, leaning on the back of the leather chaise.

Jerry nudged him in the shoulder. "Why you gotta make marriage sound so dyer by referring to it as taking the plunge? I happen to like married life."

Liam shook his head and laughed. "Says the man who vowed to never settle down with one woman."

Jerry shrugged and grin. "When the right one comes along…folks change."

"For the record, I don't have a problem with marriage," Nick explained. "I can't even imagine my life without Sumeera and our girls. I'm just wondering when Liam is going to join the club. After a while, the bachelor's life gets old.

"Don't rush him," Nate piped in. "Marriage is a serious commitment, but like these guys, I wouldn't change anything about my life. I'm sure when the right woman comes along, Liam will—"

"Maybe she's already come along, and he's too much of an idiot to realize it." Jerry stared at Liam.

Nate looked back and forth between them. "Hmm...I sense there's a story here, and if it wasn't almost eleven o'clock, I'd pry for details. But we gotta get out of here."

"Yeah, go. Bye." Liam jogged across the room and opened the door, more than ready to end the conversation and get them out of there before it started up again.

Nate laughed as he strolled toward him, his keys jingling in his hands. "Okay, so there's *definitely* a story there. You see how fast he's trying to get us out of here?"

"Yeah, and I'm almost curious enough to sit back down and demand details." Nick approached and gave Liam a fist bump. "Holler at me before you head to New York."

"Will do," he said as Nick and Nate walked out of the house. But then he shoved Jerry when he got closer. "I ought to beat your ass for trying to get something started."

Jerry burst out laughing and shoved him back. "Don't hate because you know I'm right. You gon' mess around and let someone else scoop in and snatch her. I'm just sayin'." With those parting words, Jerry left and hurried to the driveway where Nick's truck was parked. He had barely climbed into the back seat before the vehicle started moving.

As they pulled away, Liam thought about the evening and how much fun it had been hanging out with the guys. Now that they were all married, the days of kicking back and watching a game or playing poker were becoming more and more rare.

71

Liam stepped back and started closing the door, but stopped when he noticed the white Lexus sitting in front of the house. *It couldn't be,* he thought, recognizing Charlee's car.

The windows were tinted, but not too dark. He could tell someone was in the driver's seat.

There was a light breeze, and the temperature had dropped to the low seventies, but it was still a little warm out to be sitting inside a car with the windows raised. He stood there for a moment, watching to see if she'd move, or at least get out of the car. She didn't.

He spent the next few seconds debating with himself. Should he close his door and pretend she wasn't out there? Or should he go to the car and see what she wanted? And why the hell was she sitting outside in her car, at that time of night anyway? He lived in a fairly safe, family-friendly neighborhood, but still.

When a light drizzle started to fall, Liam released a low growl of frustration under his breath and headed to her car. He didn't know what he'd say to her but knew they needed to work out whatever was going on between them. And there was definitely something happening between them.

As Liam approached the vehicle, he figured Charlee would open the door and tell him why she was there. She didn't.

What the hell is going on with this woman?

As he rounded the back of the car, unease crept through his body as he slowly approached the driver's side door.

Maybe he'd been wrong. Maybe it wasn't her car.

The thought fled his mind when the street lamp illuminated just enough light for him to see inside of the window that was partially down. Her head was slumped to the side, and a lock of her hair had fallen into her face. It looked as if she was asleep.

At least he hoped she was asleep.

"Charlee?" he called out, but she didn't move. He said her name again and still, nothing.

A wave a panic swept over Liam as he rushed to check the door handle, relieved to find the door unlock. That initial panic morphed into full-blown fear now that he was inside the car. Ignoring the loud beeping that signaled her keys were in the ignition, he placed two fingers on the side of her neck, praying he'd feel a pulse.

The strong thumps pulsing against his fingers had him dropping his head and closing his eyes.

Thank you, God.

For the next few seconds, he maintained that position. What would he have done if...

No. I'm not finishing that thought.

Liam lifted his head, and a pent-up breath whooshed out of his mouth when he stood to his full height. The light drizzle of rain was doing nothing to squelch the anxiety that still roared inside of him.

He placed his hand on his chest, blowing out a noisy breath as if that would take his pounding heart back down to a normal rate. He couldn't remember the last time he'd been that scared, and he hoped he never experienced anything like that again.

A few more seconds ticked by before relief flooded through his body like water crushing through a dam. It was then that his attention went back to the irritating beeping.

He leaned over and pulled the key from the ignition, immediately silencing the car. Pocketing the set of keys, he returned his attention to his sleeping beauty.

"Charlee." He shook her shoulder, gently at first, then a little harder before she finally stirred. But still, she didn't open her eyes.

She had always slept like the dead. There had been plenty of occasions where he'd had to carry her to bed after she fell asleep on the sofa or at the kitchen table. She worked hard, played hard, and when she did finally sit down somewhere, she slept hard.

But what Liam didn't understand was why she was sleeping in the car, with a window down, key in the ignition, and the door unlocked.

"Charlee." He gently cupped her chin and pushed a few strands of her hair away as he turned her face toward him. "Sweetheart, wake up."

She finally started moving and moaned. It took a few seconds, but her eyes fluttered several times until she eventually opened those gorgeous brown eyes. She remained perfectly still except her gaze darting back and forth. Liam couldn't tell if she was really seeing anything.

"Charlee?"

Her head jerked toward him, and perfectly arched brows dipped into a frown.

"Liam? Wh—what are you doing?" she said in a hoarse whisper, barely able to keep her eyes open.

"I should be asking you the same thing."

He brushed his forearm across his forehead, wiping some of the rain away. Thankfully, it was still just a mist and hadn't started pouring.

"Why are you sitting in the car…outside of my house?"

"I—I…" She looked out the front windshield again, then glanced around the inside of her vehicle as if trying to figure that out herself. Her head dropped back against the seat, and she blew out a breath. "I—I don't know. I'm just…I think I should go home."

"I don't think so. There's no way I'm letting you drive. Come on, let's get you inside. It's starting to rain."

He stuck the key back into the ignition and raised the window before grabbing her handbag and helping her out of the car. He placed an arm around her, surprised when her head dropped to his shoulder as he guided her into the house.

"How long have you been sitting out there?" he asked, locking the door behind them, and maintaining the hold he had around her as they stood in the foyer.

"I don't know." She wobbled on unsteady legs. "I have to take off my shoes."

Charlee held onto his arm with a death grip as she kicked off her ridiculously high heels. She was still wearing the white dress that she'd had on earlier. Not many people could go the whole day wearing white and still look clean and unruffled.

"I'm so tired." She staggered, holding his arm tighter.

"Clearly. Let me help you to the living room." He untangled himself from her grip and slipped his arm around her narrow waist again.

Liam wasn't sure what to make of her being at his place, but he'd be lying if he said that he wasn't happy to see her. He just didn't like the thought of her being outside. What if he hadn't noticed her car? How long would she have slept out there?

"Have you been drinking?" he asked, concerned that something more might've been wrong with her than just exhaustion. He didn't smell alcohol on her, but wanted to rule that out. She wasn't a drinker, at least not when they were together. Sure, she'd have a drink occasionally, but nothing more than a glass of wine here and there.

"No. I'm just...I'm just a little tired."

"*A little?* You don't know how long you've been sleeping in your car and you can barely walk. I'd say you're beyond a little tired. Are you sick? Do you feel okay?"

Charlee didn't respond as he sat her on the sofa. She immediately laid her head on one of the pillows, curling into a fetal position. Her eyes drifted shut.

Befuddled, Liam placed the back of his hand on her forehead to determine if she had a fever. She might've been a little warm, but not hot enough for alarm. Noting that she had gotten a little wet, he retrieved a towel and a blanket from the linen closet. When he returned, Charlee was fast asleep, soft snores mingling with the sounds coming from the television.

He sat on the edge of the sofa and dried her face before running the towel over her bare arms. Once he finished, he covered her with the lightweight blanket.

Questions bombarded his mind as he studied this adorable, unpredictable woman. She was the queen of throwing him off balance. She was also the one person who could pull him out of a funk and then piss him off in the next minute. And though Liam wasn't the type of man who laughed a lot, he had never smiled and laughed as much as he did when she was around.

God, he missed her.

Breaking off their engagement and walking away from what they once shared had been the hardest thing he'd ever done. There had been days when he called himself all types of a fool for letting her go. Then other days he knew it had been for the best.

But had it been? Had giving up on her...on them, been for the best?

He ran his hand over his mustache and down his beard not knowing how to answer either of those questions. At least he could finally admit that he still had feelings for her and they were stronger than ever. However, right now, that was the last thing he should be thinking about.

Why was she there? Had something happened to her? She seemed fine, except for the fact that she couldn't keep her eyes open.

Liam reached over and pulled out the hairpins and a hair-thingy that had been holding the long tresses on top of her head. The thick strands fell like waves around her shoulder, a few landing over her face. Unable to resist, he weaved his fingers through the satiny curls before pushing some of the strands behind her ear.

She's mine. She will always be mine.

The thought shocked him, even though it shouldn't. He had known a couple of years ago, shortly after meeting Charlee, that she was *the one*. It didn't matter how he tried fighting his feelings, or how he hadn't planned on falling in love, it had happened within days of meeting this wild woman. Maybe Jerry was right. Maybe it was time to stop fighting his feelings.

Still studying Charlee, Liam glided the back of his knuckles down her soft cheek, something he used to do often. Why had she come to him? Had she been experiencing the same type of confusion about them that had been torturing him? Or had she come by to chew him out for acting like a barbarian earlier?

Either way, he was glad she was there. At least he knew she was safe. Considering how exhausted she was, she could've been in a car accident, hurting herself or someone else.

But she's safe.

And she's here.

At the moment, that's all that mattered.

Chapter Ten

Charlee heard talking in the distance and then cheering, but couldn't seem to lift her heavy eyelids. Instead, she snuggled deeper into the pillow and under the covers, willing herself to fall back to sleep.

But then there was more cheering.

She eased her eyes open and lowered the covers to below her chin, slowly turning onto her back. Above her was a tall coffered ceiling with dark gray squares and white beams. Confused, her gaze darted around the space. A ray of sunshine peeked through the slats of the partially opened window blinds. White walls were graced with colorful abstract art, and the source of the noise—a women's basketball game playing on the largest television she'd ever seen.

Memories of the night before came rushing to the forefront of Charlee's mind.

A dinner party hosted by her father.

Her administrative assistant's wild birthday party at a local bar.

Liam's house.

Liam.

From the moment she'd left the coffee shop, her mind had been on him. It hadn't mattered that the day had been a flurry of activity surrounded by people. He'd been the person she hadn't been able to stop thinking about. Which was how she ended up at his house. Granted, it hadn't been the best idea to just show up. Yet, it was as if an invisible force drew her to his place.

Now, here she was, laying on his sofa with him sitting near her feet. His head was back against the leather sofa, and his eyes were closed. Some parts of the night before, where he had found her in her car, were a little spotty. She remembered how patient he'd been in getting her into the house. Unfortunately, anything after that was a blur. Considering they weren't on the best of terms, it was kind of him to bring her into his home and let her sleep.

The attractive, complex man, always managed to surprise her, but how would he react once he woke up? Maybe leaving while he was asleep would be the smartest thing to do. Otherwise, she might do something stupid, like climb onto his lap, and kiss him senseless.

That could be fun.

Nah, that would be too much even for her. Besides, she wanted them to call a truce. She was tired of tiptoeing around him whenever they were in the same space, or being on the receiving end of one of his evil glares.

Then again, instead of sneaking out, maybe she'd just lay there and get her fill of his handsome face. Considering how intense he could be, he looked so relaxed and calm when he slept.

A smile touched her lips, and a sweet thrill filled her at his closeness. He could've easily left her in the living room and retired to his bedroom, but he hadn't. He had stayed there…with her. That meant more to Charlee than he'd ever know. He cared. He still cared about her, and it made her want to leap off the sofa and do a few cartwheels.

It blew her mind the type of effect that one man could have on her. She'd dated some nice guys from all walks of life over the years. Wealthy, good-looking, entrepreneurs, and even a president of a bank, but not one of them made her feel complete. Not the way she felt whenever she was with Liam.

But what would happen when he awakened? She hadn't had a solid plan when parking in front of his house. She would've rang the doorbell had there not been a huge truck in his driveway. Assuming that he had company, she had decided to sit in her car a few minutes until they were gone, then ring his doorbell.

Well, that didn't work out.

"Knowing you, I'm sure you're probably hungry."

Charlee startled at Liam's sleep-filled baritone and gripped the blanket tighter.

"French toast all right with you?" he asked.

How long had he been awake? He hadn't moved and even now, his eyes were closed. And how had he known she was awake? She hadn't really moved.

Then another thought pierced her mind and a spark of hope shot through her like fireworks shooting through the sky on the Fourth of July. If he still hated her, no way would he offer to feed her, and now that he mentioned it, she was starving.

"If I get a choice, I'd prefer lasagna."

His eyes popped open, and he looked at her, a slight frown creasing his forehead. "How'd you know I made lasagna yesterday?"

Her brows shot up. "I—I didn't know," she sputtered, surprised and happy to hear that. "But now that I know, can I have some?"

His lasagna was the best that Charlee had ever eaten, and from the first time he'd cooked for her, she'd been a goner. She had always had a healthy appetite, which was perfect in their case. Liam loved to cook. With his culinary skills, he could easily succeed at owning a restaurant. He had once told her that all the men in his family were good cooks, which blew Charlee's mind. Just another reason why the Jenkins men were the most eligible bachelors in the city. At least they used to be. So many of them, the ones she knew of thanks to Rayne, had been snatched up already.

A sudden hollowness settled in her chest. Liam's family and the fact that he had never formally introduced her to any of them used to be a source of contention between them. Though she knew he was a private man, she never understood why he always found an excuse to not take her around them. Granted, she traveled more than she was at home, but he'd had a few opportunities. According to him, it was because he didn't want them in his business, but Charlee always wondered if it was for other reasons.

"You coming?" Liam asked, standing next to the sofa. So caught up in her thoughts, she hadn't realized he moved.

She quickly placed her feet on the floor, the hardwood cool against her soles. "Uh, yeah."

"There's a toothbrush in the guest bathroom, top drawer on the right-hand side, and your gym bag is over there," he pointed to a nearby chair. "Anything else you need, check the linen closet. Make yourself at home. I'm gonna go shower. Then I'll meet you in the kitchen." He headed down the hallway toward the master bedroom without a backward glance.

Charlee sat there dumbfounded. What happened to the fickle, ornery man she had grown accustomed to over the past year? She glanced at the gym bag, glad she made a habit of keeping a change of clothes in her trunk, but for him to get it for her sometime during the night, meant everything.

Her heart fluttered inside of her chest. This was the man she had fallen in love with years ago. Liam was the most giving man she knew, and when they were together, he took care of her. Whether it was making sure she ate, ensuring that she arrived at a destination safely, or just reading her mood and acting accordingly.

No one had ever taken care of her the way he had, except for maybe her father and Rayne. But with Liam, it was different. He used to make her feel as if she was the most important person in the world. Even now, though they weren't together and he could have easily escorted her out of his house, he hadn't. Instead, he made her feel comfortable.

With her heart and mind doing funny things, Charlee grabbed her bag bewildered by Liam's actions. Maybe there was a chance that they could at least be friends again. As she strolled across the living room toward the hallway that led to the guest bathroom, she took note of the changes Liam had made to the house.

He had purchased the three-bedroom, two-bathroom ranch home shortly before they'd started dating. It hadn't needed much work, but it looked as if he had made substantial changes. There had been a wall that separated the living room, dining room, and kitchen. It was gone. Dark hardwoods had replaced the old shag carpet, and the dated light fixtures had been swapped out by more modern ones.

Charlee walked into the guest bathroom that had also received a face lift. The black and white decor was replaced with a brown and beige color pallet and a new vanity.

"Wow. Fancy, fancy," she said, as she admired the dual shower heads in the glass enclosed shower. She couldn't wait to test out some of the settings.

Twenty minutes later, Charlee was refreshed and had changed into a pair of yoga pants and a fitted T-shirt. Once she had wrangled her curls into a ponytail, she left the bathroom and dropped her bag off in the front foyer.

The smell of coffee greeted her, immediately bringing back more memories of the past. She wasn't a big coffee drinker, but Liam never started the day without at least one, obscenely strong cup of the dark liquid. She wondered what else had stayed the same about him.

"What would you like to drink?" he said from the stove where he had bacon as well as French toast going. Charlee spied the pan holding lasagna on the counter near the refrigerator.

"Do you have any tea?" she asked, doubting he'd have any, but preferring that over coffee.

"Green or herbal?"

Her brows shot up. "You have tea? A man who practically inhales coffee actually has tea?"

He gave a slight shrug and pulled a variety pack box of tea from the well-stocked pantry. "I fixed breakfast for Jada and my mother for Valentine's Day. My mom likes tea. So, what's your pleasure?"

What's my pleasure? Now that's a dangerous question, Charlee thought as her gaze raked over the blue T-shirt that hugged his broad chest and muscular biceps. Dark jeans covered his legs and hung low on his hips. He looked comfortable and sexy all rolled into one. If she had to choose which part of him she wanted, she'd prefer to have the whole package.

Liam gave the tea box a little shake, forcing her eyes back up to his face. His tempting lips quirked. "When I asked the question, I was referring to the tea. What type do you want?"

Charlee's attention bounced between him and the box. "Oh. Green tea is good." *And a big dose of you to take home with me would be great.* But she kept that thought to herself as she sat at the small kitchen table.

He wasn't only a wonderful man. He was also a good brother and son. Charlee didn't know any men who prepared breakfast for their mother and sister...and her.

How could she have chosen so wrong? She should've been married with kids *and* a successful career. But back then, she didn't know how to have it all. Juggling work and Liam had proved to be harder than she thought. She hadn't had sense enough to cut back on some of her hours in order to save her relationship.

Liam placed a steaming cup of tea in front of her and then a plate of lasagna and a piece of garlic bread. Charlee inhaled the enticing aroma and quickly dug in. It was so good, her eyes drifted closed as she chewed and a moan slipped through.

"As good as I remember."

Liam set his breakfast and coffee on the table before sitting across from her. "Glad you think so. There's more if you're still hungry."

They ate in silence, and surprisingly it wasn't uncomfortable, but Charlee knew he was probably curious about why she was there.

"About last night..." she started, but stopped to find the words that would best explain why she showed up on his doorstep out of the blue.

"Yeah, let's talk about that. What were you thinking, falling asleep in your car with the key in the ignition? Not only that, the window was down and the driver's door was unlocked? Do you know how dangerous that was? Do you have *any* idea how much you scared the crap out of me?"

Okay, so the conversation wasn't going the way she envisioned it in her head, but she didn't miss the anguish and concern in his voice.

"It wasn't my intention to fall asleep. I wanted to talk to you, but when I saw the truck in your driveway and all the lights on, I figured you had company. I had planned to wait for a few minutes to see if they left, but...I guess I was more tired than I thought."

Actually, she knew she was tired after leaving the bar, but her need to see Liam had outweighed the desire to go home and climb into bed.

"Had you been drinking?"

"I had a glass of wine at my father's house during a dinner party and a glass of wine at a birthday party that I attended last night. I wasn't drunk and felt fine to drive."

"Yet, you fell asleep in your car. What was so important that you had to see me? And why not just call if you wanted to talk?"

"I didn't want you to hang up on me," she said quietly, sounding pitiful to her own ears. She handled million-dollar deals, managed hundreds of staff, and was a grown-ass woman. Yet she was afraid that the man sitting across from her would hang up on her if she called.

"I wouldn't have hung up on you," Liam said after a long silence.

Charlee eyed him as he continued eating, waiting for him to say more, but he didn't. How was she supposed to know that he wouldn't have hung up? He'd been such a contradiction the last few times they'd run into each other. She hadn't been sure what to expect.

"So what do you want?" he asked pointedly, staring at her over the rim of his mug.

You. All I want is you.

Instead of saying that, she said, "You know what I want."

His left brow rose toward the ceiling, but he didn't respond as he continued studying her.

Ugh. She hated when he looked at her like that. Like he was picking through her mind, searching for the meaning of her existence.

She snatched a napkin from the silver holder on the table and wiped her mouth. "I want a truce, all right? I'm tired of the tension between us every time we run into each other, and I hate it when you look at me as if I'm some...some alien who's trying to steal your kidney."

He lowered the mug to the table and shook his head. His lips twitched before giving way to a slight smile and a chuckle. "You're something else."

"I'm not done. I also want us to be friends again. I miss you, Liam. Even if we never get back what we once had, you have to admit that we were once good friends."

His smile disappeared, and he sat back in his seat, folding his arms across his chest. "I agree."

Whoa. She hadn't expected that and stared at him, waiting for him to continue. Secretly, she yearned for him to tell her that he was madly in love with her. How he couldn't go another day without her in his life. And once that was said, Charlee wanted him to pull her into his arms and kiss her until she couldn't think straight.

85

When none of that happened, she asked, "You agree? To which part?"

After a long hesitation, he said, "All of it."

Chapter Eleven

Okaaay. What does that mean?

There were so many things Charlee loved about this man, but those same things irritated the hell out of her. Like for instance, he wasn't a big talker, often letting his actions speak louder than words. However, when she needed him to say something, anything, he took his time and often didn't share his thoughts without her prying them out of him.

"All of what?" she asked as he stood and started clearing the table. "Are you saying that you agree that you've been treating me like an alien?"

"Yes."

Frustration drummed through her. "And you want to call a truce?"

Instead of loading the dishwasher, he started washing the dishes. "Yes."

"And you want us to be friends? Like hanging out sometimes like we used to?" she continued carefully, mentally, and emotionally preparing herself for however he answered. He continued washing and drying dishes, seeming to marinate on each question.

"Yes," he finally said.

"And you miss me?"

"Dammit, Charlee!" He threw the dish towel on the counter, suds flying everywhere. "Yes! What else do you want me to say? Yes! I agree with all of that."

Charlee stood within an arm's reach of him, her mouth hanging open at his outburst, unsure of what to say. The words out of his mouth were everything she wanted to hear, but the tension radiating off him and the tortured look on his face was saying something completely different.

"You...your presence. Heck, everything about you turns me on and confuses the hell out of me. You drive me...crazy! Yeah, that's it. You drive me crazy, all right?" He angrily dried his hands. "Is that what you wanted to hear? Because that's how you make me feel. Like...like I'm losing my damn mind! I can't stop thinking about you, and it's making me nuts. I miss the hell out of you, okay? Now stop with all of the questions!"

Breathing hard, he white-knuckled gripped the edge of the counter and hung his head as if it had taken every bit of energy he had to admit that to her.

A slow smile spread across Charlee's mouth. Surely, he knew telling her to stop doing something was like telling her to go for it. Most people would be sympathetic to the apparent battle going on inside of him. She wasn't most people. Happiness bubbled inside of her at the thought that she was making him crazy.

Served him right. The way she'd been missing him had been just as much torture, and she was glad he'd been experiencing it, too. Heck, she was so elated, a happy dance on top of the counter in only her underwear seemed in order. But she wouldn't. At least not today.

"Okay, now that we got that out in the open, let's talk."

He whipped his head around so fast it was a wonder it didn't roll off of his neck.

"Are you kidding me? We just talked. *I* just talked."

Charlee burst out laughing. She laughed even harder when he rolled his eyes and poured himself another cup of coffee. If it was left up to Liam, he'd probably never talk.

"Okay, okay, I'll do the talking and you'll listen, something you're really good at anyway. But there's just one thing."

Just as he brought the mug up to his lips, Charlee took it from him and set it on the counter next to the stove. She tugged on the front of his shirt, and Liam lifted a questioning brow but allowed her to pull him closer. His dark, piercing eyes met hers.

They wanted the same thing.

Her body hummed with need and her nipples tightened at the burning desire illuminating in his eyes. When his gaze volleyed from her eyes to her mouth, Charlee couldn't resist any longer. She raised up on tiptoe and gently pressed her lips to his, anxious to see if that spark that they once shared was still there.

A jolt of electricity raced over her skin and excitement pulsed through her veins as her senses leaped to life.

Yep, that spark is still there.

She might've started the kiss, but Liam quickly took over. One of his strong arms encircled her waist and he pulled her tight against his body while his other hand gripped the back of her neck. His tongue swept into her mouth with a soul-reaching urgency that had Charlee gripping the back of his shirt, holding on for dear life.

She wasn't surprised by her own eager response. Each time she'd seen him, she'd wanted to kiss him, taste him, be reminded of how perfect his mouth felt against hers. She wanted to be locked in his arms again and finally, finally she was right where she wanted to be if only for a minute.

When the kiss ended, a whoosh of air burst from her lungs and Charlee steadied herself, trying to exude some level of coolness. She didn't want him to see how much the kiss affected her.

The left corner of his juicy lips quirked up. "I wondered if you'd taste the same," he said huskily.

"Well, did I?" she asked, her voice shakier than she would've preferred.

His gaze lowered to her mouth and settled there for a while before reaching her eyes again. "I think I need another sample before I can form an official answer."

He pulled her body tight to his, her breasts pressed firmly against his hard chest. His hands slid slowly down the side of her body, scorching everywhere he touched before settling on her hips.

Oh yeah, this was what she needed, what she desired more than anything. Things might not be settled between them, but if the kisses were any indication, they were officially waving the white flag. Their truce was secure.

Liam moaned and held her tighter as if he couldn't get enough of her. A wave a power engulfed Charlee. It was nice to know she still affected him mentally and physically.

Sparks of desire roared through her body, but reality knocked inside of her head. This was just a kiss. Steamy. Hot. Delicious. But it was just a kiss. All it proved was that they were still very much attracted to each other. They still needed to talk, to discuss the past that had ultimately affected them both.

She whimpered when she had to slide her lips from his. *I want you so bad,* teetered on her tongue, but she kept those words to herself. She had pretty thick skin, but Liam had the power to knock her down a peg or two with very few words. The last thing she wanted was to move too fast or say anything that would make him return to glaring at her.

Charlee backed out of his hold. "Let's talk. I mean, I'll talk and you can listen."

She returned to the kitchen chair that she had vacated and watched his every move. As if he had all the time in the world, he placed his coffee mug in the microwave and turned it on. He also heated more water in the kettle, and Charlee assumed it was to top off her tea.

Was he intentionally taking his time to join her at the table? He knew she wanted to discuss their history. Did his hesitance mean that she had read too much into his admission of missing her? But why not just ask her to leave if he didn't want to discuss their past?

Liam scooped up the last of the lasagna and put it in a plastic container before placing it in a small paper bag. Instead of just telling her that it was for her, he pointed between her and the bag that he'd set on the edge of the counter. He really was a thoughtful guy even if he acted like a barbarian at times.

Finally, he joined her at the table with their drinks. "Talk," he said gruffly, and Charlee struggled to keep from rolling her eyes.

He might've worn a tough, I-don't-give-a-damn attitude, but she knew the man behind the mask. The man who could be sweet, caring, thoughtful while still exuding a masculine power that would make others think twice about stepping to him with some nonsense.

Charlee wrapped her hands around the mug and stared into the liquid as if it would give her courage and the words needed to start this conversation. She already knew that if she didn't say anything, Liam could sit there for hours staring at her without mumbling a word. Then they still wouldn't be any closer to shutting and locking the door of the past to make room for something even more spectacular in the future.

"I'm sorry for the way things ended between us," Charlee finally said. "Despite what you thought, I wanted to marry you. I wanted, and had planned to spend the rest of my days with you, and I hate that I didn't fight to keep you in my life."

She chanced a glance at him. His elbows were on the table, his mug was near his mouth, and his unwavering attention was solely on her. Anybody else would jump in and say something at this point, but not him. At least he was listening. In the past when she tried apologizing for how things turned out, he wouldn't let her say the words before changing the subject or walking away.

Charlee inhaled and released a slow, calming breath. She was hesitant to put her heart out there. She wanted another chance, wanted him to give them another chance to prove what she already knew. They belonged together. But maybe it would be best if she focused on them being friends and regaining his trust. She'd rather have him as a friend than not have him in her life at all. Yet, she still felt a need to explain why her career was so important to her.

She blew on the tea before taking a careful sip. "I always wanted to be a successful businesswoman. Prove to myself and others that I was capable of making a thriving company even more profitable. However, I didn't mean to put my career before you. I thought I could have a great job, you, and a family. Clearly, I didn't know how to juggle everything. I actually thought I could have it all."

"You can have it all," Liam said, and Charlee's head jerked up. "What I mean is that you can have the life that you desire. It's all about balance, setting priorities, and being committed to what's important. Only you can decide what's important to you."

Charlee studied him, shocked that he'd said that much. She was also trying to decipher what else he was really saying behind those carefully worded words.

"Are you saying I wasn't committed to us? That you weren't important to me?"

"I think you wanted to be committed to what we were building, but your career was more important." Charlee started shaking her head, but he lifted his hand to stop her from speaking. "You wanted to prove to yourself and to your father that you had what it took to run the company. I understood that. What I couldn't get with was you *always* putting work before me."

A stab of pain pierced Charlee's chest and she broke eye contact. He was right. She was on a mission to learn every aspect of Fenlon Manufacturing for the purpose of one day running the company. Her father would never let her slide

92

into a leadership position. She had to earn it. She had to prove that she was worthy and could actually do the job.

"I loved you, and there is nothing I wouldn't have done for you," Liam said quietly, almost as if he was talking to himself.

Charlee returned her attention to him. Seeing hurt in his eyes was almost her undoing, and she swallowed, batting her eyes several times to keep her tears at bay.

"But after we were engaged, you canceled on me one too many times. I was prepared for all of the traveling, even agreed to go with you sometimes. When you weren't ready to set a date for the wedding, I was fine with that. As long as I knew you would one day be my wife, that was all that mattered. We talked about when we'd start a family, and you said you wanted to wait at least five years. I could live with that. I was prepared to do whatever necessary to have you in my life."

Liam cleared his throat and ran his hand over his mouth and several minutes ticked by without him speaking. Charlee wanted him to say what hadn't been said back then.

"One cancellation turned into another, then another, then another. It was clear then that you and I weren't on the same page. I'm a firm believer that however a relationship starts, that's how it will end up. I didn't want to always be an afterthought, and you weren't ready for what I was ready for which was marriage and starting a family."

But I'm ready now, Charlee wanted to say but remained quiet. It wasn't easy being reminded of how the end of their relationship played out. When he'd asked her to marry him, it had come out of nowhere, but saying yes had been a no-brainer. She loved him completely and had no doubt that he loved her.

At first, she hadn't realized that she was putting him second. She also hadn't realized just how many events, dinners, or even date nights she'd had to cancel on. It wasn't until Liam had surprised her and showed up at the hotel during one of her business trips in Minnesota did she realize something was wrong. She had been so happy to see him until he started pointing out how much she had missed. He broke off their engagement, claiming she didn't love him enough.

Charlee reached over and covered his hand with hers and squeezed. "I'm sorry. I am so sorry I took you and your love for granted. Please believe me when I say that I loved you then, and I will always love you, Liam."

His eyes searched hers before he spoke again. "We can't go back. We'll never be able to go back to what we had."

Charlee eased her hand from his as her heart plummeted to her stomach. Raw hurt and terrible regrets filled the empty cavity between her ribs and she fought to keep tears at bay. Without a word, she rushed from the kitchen and hurried down the hall to the bathroom, refusing to be humiliated any more than she already had been.

I am such a fool.

Chapter Twelve

Ah hell.

Liam ran after her, but before he reached the hallway, the bathroom door slammed. This was why he preferred listening over talking, especially when he spoke before thinking. Why couldn't he have kept his thoughts to himself?

"Charlee, open the door." When she didn't respond, and he didn't hear any movement, he checked the doorknob and found the door unlocked. "I'm coming in," he said as he eased the door open.

She was sitting on the cushioned bench, her head down and a crumpled tissue in her hand. Charlee wasn't an overly sensitive woman, which meant he had really screwed up. How did he keep getting into these situations? He didn't go around hurting women. Yet, in a matter of forty-eight hours, he'd managed to do just that with two women he cared deeply for.

He snatched a couple of tissues from the Kleenex box on the vanity and sat next to her, hoping the bench could hold them both. He swapped out her used tissue for the clean ones, tossing the crumbled ones in the nearby trash can.

"Thank you." She dabbed at her eyes.

"Listen, I'm sorry for what I said. I'm an insensitive idiot."

"I agree, but I know you can't help it."

A slow smile spread across Liam's mouth and he shook his head. He meant it when he'd told her that he missed her. His life was more balanced and exciting when she was in it. He also didn't have as many restless nights and frustrated days.

But this woman...

This woman had the ability to turn his life upside down and inside out, and if he wasn't careful, he'd end up right where he'd been almost two years ago. There were too many times with her that he acted out of character, doing and saying things that he wouldn't normally do.

Liam cringed inside as a few of those memories came to the forefront in his mind. Like the time when they were out of town at a night club and a guy who'd had too much to drink got handsy with her. Liam punched him, breaking his nose. Or the time they were waiting to board a flight out of Hartsfield-Jackson Atlanta airport, and she dared him to tell the world that he loved her. He had talked airport personnel into letting him announce his love for Charlee over the loudspeaker.

Liam leaned forward, his elbows on his thighs. There were times he didn't recognize himself where Charlee was concerned. Yet, he liked how he was when they were together. She loosened him up, forced him to step out of the carefully constructed wall he'd built around himself, and challenged him to live out loud. Left up to him, he'd be totally comfortable alone on a deserted island as long as he could sketch and watch sports. Charlee, on the other hand, loved life, people, and was always up for an adventure.

And he loved her.

Last night he had finally admitted it to himself. He was still in love with Charlee. Even knowing that though, he would never let her take advantage of him or his love again. But he had to find some happy medium regarding his feelings for her.

"What I should've said in the kitchen was that, though we can't go back and fix or redo the past, I'd like for us to at least be friends."

Charlee lifted her head and narrowed her red eyes. "Really? You want to be friends…with me? Even though I took you for granted? Even though I didn't fight for you…for us?"

He grinned and bumped shoulders with her. "Yeah, even with all of that. To be honest, it wasn't all on you. I could've done a better job communicating."

She nodded and stared down at the floor. "Would've, should've, could've. That's how life goes. Well, I'm glad we talked and got a few things out in the open."

Yeah, some things were out in the open, but Liam wasn't ready to tell her how he felt about her. Heck, he was still trying to come to grips with that knowledge himself.

What did it mean to still be in love with her? Could he take a chance on getting involved with her again? Was he just a glutton for punishment? Or could he ignore his strong feelings for her, keep his distance, and live the rest of his life wondering what could have been?

Good thing he was heading out of town in a couple of days. It was the perfect opportunity to get away and get his head on straight. Maybe by the time he returned, he'd know what to do about Charlee. He meant what he said about them not being able to pick up where they left off, but that didn't mean that they couldn't start fresh.

"I should probably get going." She stood, tossing the tissue in the trash. "I hope I didn't ruin your day."

"You didn't." Liam reached for her hand. "Come here."

She stepped into his embrace without hesitation. Kissing the side of her head, Liam held her close, breathing in her fresh scent and reveling in the feel of her being in his arms again. He really had missed her, and if he was truly honest with himself, he wanted her back in his life.

"I didn't mean to make you cry," he said close to her ear.

"I know. I won't hold it against you, especially since you said I make you crazy."

A chuckle vibrated inside of him. He missed her humor. "But even so, just know that I care about you. I never want to say or do anything to hurt you. Okay?"

"Okay."

Liam wasn't sure how long they stood there holding each other. Even when he heard his cell phone ringing, he didn't let her go.

Charlee lifted her head and looked up at him. Her mouth was only inches from his and Liam wanted more than anything to kiss her again, but he wouldn't. At least not yet. Not until he came to grips with what he felt for her.

"Are you going to answer that?" she asked. His cell phone was ringing again.

"No, but I should let you get going." He reluctantly dropped his arms, and they made their way out of the bathroom. When they were near the front door, Liam snapped his finger. "Almost forgot. Let me go grab your lasagna." When he returned, he handed her the bag.

"Thank you, and thanks for last night," she said with a grin, her voice husky, her words suggestive.

Liam shook his head and returned her smile. "I would say anytime, but no more driving when you're that tired, and definitely no sleeping in your car. If you come by again, even if you think I have company, ring the doorbell."

She nodded. "I'll remember that. Now that I know I drive you crazy—"

"I'm already sorry I ever told you that." Liam opened the door and leaned his shoulder against it.

"I'm not. As a matter of fact, instead of heading home and getting ready for a new work week, I should stick around and see how much crazier I can make you." She strolled out the door. "Maybe another day?"

Liam laughed. "Yeah, sure, why not? Until then."

She smiled and gave a small wave. "Until then."

*

Humming along with the song flowing through her computer speakers, Charlee signed the documents that had been left on her desk. Rarely did she use her personal days, but after her eventful weekend, she had taken Monday and Tuesday off. She couldn't stop thinking about Liam. Listening to him Saturday, she understood better just how much she had hurt him.

Charlee tossed her pen down and leaned back against her chair.

"What am I going to do? I want him back," she mumbled, wishing he'd give them another chance. He'd had every right to break off their engagement. Liam loved hard, and like with everything, he gave one-hundred percent to their relationship. Getting married and having a family of his own was what he wanted. He'd made that clear early on and she had wanted that, too.

Then what happened? Why couldn't she get it right?

If only he would've given her time to figure out how to juggle him and her crazy schedule back then. No matter how she tried to assure him that he meant everything to her, it hadn't been enough. According to him, those had been just words. Her actions spoke louder.

If given another chance, she would definitely do things differently. Her work didn't keep her warm at night or fill that lonely void in her heart. If only she had known that back then.

When you know better, you do better, she thought, placing the signed documents in her outgoing tray for her assistant. All she needed was a chance to show him that she wasn't the same person.

Charlee placed her hands palms down on her desk, determined to focus on work. "Okay. I need to get something done today."

She glanced at her schedule and zoned in on the word *presentation* written in big, bold letters. Her trip to New York to present to the Richardson group was coming up quick and there was so much riding on her proposal. She had to bring home a win.

She pressed the intercom button.

"Yes?" her assistant said.

"Emery, can you hold my calls?"

"Of course."

"Thank you."

For the next hour, Charlee made changes to her PowerPoint presentation. Trying to convince the Richardson group to use Fenlon as their exclusive vendor wasn't going to be easy, but she had a deal for them they wouldn't be able to resist.

Her cell phone chimed, signaling a text message. She pulled the device from the side pocket of her handbag and glanced at the message.

Liam: Hi

Charlee couldn't stop the grin from spreading across her face as giddiness blossomed inside of her. Surprised to hear from him, she couldn't type her reply fast enough.

Charlee: Hi yourself!

When seconds ticked by and he didn't respond, she typed another message.

Charlee: WYD?

She hit send, but then thought about who she was talking to. Would Liam know that WYD meant—What you doing? He barely talked on the phone. She doubted he texted often. Seconds ticked by before he responded.

Liam: Nothing

Charlee shook her head. Why'd he text her if he didn't have anything to say? Then again, giving her a shout out was a sweet gesture and meant a lot coming from him.

Charlee: How's your day going?

Liam: Fine

Charlee: We really need to work on you talking more. Or in this case, responding with more than one-word answers.

Liam: Okay

Charlee burst out laughing.

Charlee: That's it? That's all you have to say?

Liam: Yes

Charlee: LOL. Now you're just messing with me.

Liam: Maybe.

Charlee: SMH. Well, it's good hearing from you.

Again, seconds ticked by without a response. Charlee tried not to read too much into the delay, but she had to tread lightly with Liam. He might've agreed to the truce, but that didn't mean that he wanted to reunite.

Liam: Dinner. You and me. Soon

She stared at the screen in shock. *Dinner?* This was huge. She didn't want to sound anxious, but her first thought was to type—HECK YEAH. SAY WHEN! Instead, she went with something a little less desperate.

Charlee: That would be nice.

She started to tell him that she'd be out of town for a few days, but thought better of it. No sense in reminding him of the past. Back then, she was out of town more than she'd been in town. He might not believe that she didn't travel for work as much anymore. Given the chance, she'd show him that her priorities had shifted.

Charlee: How about next week sometime?

Liam: Okay. Bye

Grinning, Charlee returned the phone to her handbag. A text message and a dinner invite were more than she had expected, but she couldn't help but be hopeful. Who knew, maybe they'd find their way back to each other as more than just friends.

A knock sounded on her office door before it slid open.

"Hey, sweetheart. I see you made it in today." Her father walked further into the office, looking like the successful businessman he was in his tailored three-piece suit.

She stood, and walked around her desk and hugged him. "Hey, Dad. Yup, I'm here."

"You doing okay? I was surprised to find out you took a couple of days off. Since you didn't return my call last night, I was starting to get concerned."

"Oh, I'm fine. I was just..." Telling him that she needed a few days to lick her wounds and time to come up with a plan to win Liam back, wouldn't be a good idea. Instead, she said, "I just needed a little break."

He nodded. His keen eyes studied her in a way that made it seem that he wasn't buying her reason. It wasn't a total lie. She had needed the rest. Falling asleep in her car Saturday night was unacceptable, as well as dangerous. She was a little surprised, but relieved, that Liam hadn't given her a harder time. It wouldn't have been the first time that he accused her of being reckless with her safety.

She reclaimed her seat, and Kingslee sat in one of the guest chairs in front of her desk. "Well, you look rested. When was the last time you took an actual vacation?"

She preferred not admitting that it had been over a year.

"I'll probably plan something soon. Right now, I'm putting the finishing touches on my presentation for the Richardson group. I'm feeling good about the meeting with them later this week."

"That's actually what I came in here for. I'm sending Bradley on the trip with you."

"What? Dad, this is my project. How are you going to just assign someone else to it?"

"Technically, this is still my company. I can do whatever I see fit."

Charlee growled under her breath and disappointment lodged in her chest. "Does that mean that you don't think I'm capable of closing the deal? Have you forgotten about the millions of dollars in contracts that I have secured for *your* company?" she spat out, anger quickly replacing the disappointment.

What the heck was she going to have to do for him to see her as capable?

"Of course, I haven't forgotten what you've done for this company," he said calmly, only irritating her more. "But I know Edward. He's old school and so is their general manager. I'm sending Bradley with you just as a face...a support, but the presentation and winning this contract will all be on you. Besides, I don't like the idea of you in New York by yourself."

Charlee tapped her pen against the top of her desk. The part about her traveling alone was nonsense. Most of her business trips over the years were done alone, but he had a point about Edward Richardson. The man was still a member of the *old boy's club* and a male chauvinist. She'd dealt with him in the past, each time he pacified her with a virtual pat on the head and a small equipment purchase.

Charlee laid the pen down and sat back in her chair. Having Bradley Handler there might not be a bad idea. They worked good together, and he brought a different set of skills to the table. He could be persuasive without being pushy, a skill she was still trying to master. He also wouldn't try to take over.

"Fine, he can come. As long as he understands that this is my deal."

Chapter Thirteen

"Okay, Liam. How does this outfit look on PJ?" his sister asked, forcing him to pull his attention away from SportsCenter that he was watching on television.

"It looks just like the last three outfits."

He, his sister, Jada, and her family had flown to New York together three days ago to visit their cousin Peyton Jenkins-Cutter who lived in Brooklyn. It had been fun hanging out and catching up for the first couple of days, but now Liam was about ready to ditch them all.

He had expected his brother-in-law and Peyton's husband to be there when he returned from having breakfast with one of his old college buddies, but they had taken their sons to a nearby park. Now Liam was stuck there with the women.

"Where's Michaela?" he asked of Peyton's pre-teen daughter. Even at her age, she could give them her opinion since she loved clothes and shoes.

"She's at a birthday party," Peyton supplied. "Now, back to the outfit. How's it look? Jada designed it, and I'm thinking about modeling it in her fashion show this fall."

Liam shrugged, then returned his attention back to the TV. "It looks fine."

"Dang, Liam. Quit acting like such a guy. How does it look on her?" his sister yelled.

He laughed. "I am a guy, and for real, the shorts or skirt or whatever those are," he waved his hand dismissively, "does look the same as the thing she had on before, just a different color."

Jada threw a pillow at him. "This suit looks nothing like the other outfits, you moron."

"Fine. It looks fine, all right? And why are you torturing me with this mini-fashion show? You know I don't know anything about fashion."

"Maybe not, but you either like the outfit or you don't," Peyton said.

"Yeah, so quit being such a knucklehead and look at the outfit," Jada griped. "Besides, you don't have to know anything about clothes, but I'm sure you know what you like to see on women."

"But she's not a woman. I mean she's a woman, but she's my cousin. I can't—"

"Oh, good grief." Jada threw up her hands. "And you're supposed to be my smart, in touch brother. I might as well have Adam here if I wanted someone who could care less about anything," she said of their older brother. "Don't look at PJ like your cousin. Imagine this outfit on your woman...*if* you had a woman."

Liam's thoughts immediately went to Charlee.

Damn. He'd been doing so good at only thinking about her every few hours. Which was better than every minute like he'd been doing after texting her a couple of days ago. He had reached out on a whim, not really wanting to talk, but wanting some interaction with her and had opted for texting. She might not officially be his woman, but she was the one who held his heart.

Liam reevaluated the outfit that Peyton was wearing. Though Charlee was thinner and a little shorter, she could definitely rock the silky, gold pants suit. Well, actually, it was a shorts suit, and the shorts barely extended past the hem of the jacket. Either way, the color would look nice against Charlee's brown skin, and the shorts would show off her gorgeous legs.

Yeah, she would look hella good in the outfit.

"Okay, I like it. A lot. It's hot."

Both women stood in stunned silence, looking at him as if they didn't recognize him.

"What? I said I like it."

"Are you dating someone?" Peyton asked, folding her arms across her chest and tapping her foot, the pointy high heels making a clicking sound against the hardwood. Her stance reminded him of when she used to run Jenkins & Sons Construction. She was an electrician by trade but had managed the company like a badass boss.

But Liam had no idea why she was regarding him through narrowed eyes, and his sister looked as if she was about to explode from excitement.

"Okay, you guys lost me. No, I'm not dating anyone, and what does that have to do with anything?"

"Oh my, *God*. He is dating!" Jada screeched and dropped onto the sofa, throwing her arms around his neck. "It's about time. I was starting to lose hope, thinking you were going to grow old all by yourself."

"Whatever. Move." He tried shaking her off, but she hung on.

"Who is she? Where'd you meet? How come I haven't met her yet?"

"JJ, I'm not playin' with you. Get off of me, crazy woman. I said I wasn't dating anyone." He shook out of her hold and bolted off the sofa.

Peyton stood next to him grinning. "You were looking at the outfit as if you were picturing someone in it. Besides, you're a horrible liar. The truth is written all over your face. There's a woman in your life."

"I wonder if MJ knows," Jada said of their cousin Martina.

"I doubt it. Otherwise, the whole family would know."

106

Jada nodded. "True."

Liam kept quiet, preferring not to encourage the conversation. He couldn't help but wonder if they really did see something on his face. He wasn't lying about not dating, but thoughts of Charlee were never far from his mind. They needed to talk. They needed to figure out if there was anything left between them. He already knew his answer. She was *the one*. He just needed to know if she wanted him as much as he wanted her.

"I'm going to change clothes," Peyton announced, heading to the stairs that would take her to the second floor of their brownstone. "But when I come back, I want to hear all about her."

"Well, it's going to be a *very* short conversation. I'm not dating and there's nothing to tell." Liam grabbed the television remote and dropped down in an overstuffed chair.

"If you were dating, would you tell me?" Jada asked, still sitting on the sofa.

She crossed one leg over the other, swinging her foot that was encased in a four-inch heel yellow sandal, back and forth. He might not know anything about her yellow and white sundress or the latest fashion, but even he knew those red bottom shoes probably cost a small fortune.

Growing up the youngest of three and the only girl, Jada had been a spoiled brat. Everyone in the family indulged her love for the finer things in life, especially shoes and clothes. It was a good thing she married a wealthy man to support her champagne taste. There wasn't anything Zack wouldn't do for her. He worshiped the ground she walked on.

"So...would you have told me?" Jada asked again.

"Told you what?"

She pursed her lips and scowled. Liam loved messing with her and had no intention of telling her anything. Actually, what could he say—*I'm in love with a woman, but I'm afraid to trust her again with my heart?* Or *I'm seriously thinking about going all in to have Charlee Fenlon in my life again even if it means being second to her career.*

107

Nah, it was best he kept his feelings for her close to his chest for now.

"Well, if there is a special someone in your life and I'm sensing there is, give her a chance, Liam. Don't expect her to be perfect."

Liam opened his mouth to ask what that was supposed to mean, but Jada lifted her hand.

"I'm not done. I love you and all, but you can be kind of rigid with your holier-than-thou attitude. You're too hard on folks and sometimes your expectations aren't reasonable."

"Excuse me? Are you talking about me or you?" he asked, irritation needling its way through his body. "Because I seem to remember a time when you wanted what you wanted, and everybody else be damned."

"I've grown since then, and we're not talking about me, we're talking about you," she said haughtily. "All I'm trying to do is remind you that everyone isn't perfect. Not even you. Love is about accepting people the way they are, meeting them halfway. Sometimes it requires compromise, especially if you truly love that person."

Liam let her words sink in. He had seen her behavior and attitude transform, in a good way, over the years since marrying Zack. She was clearly speaking from experience.

"Anything else?" he asked dryly. Everything she said about him was true. He already knew his shortcomings even if they were hard to accept, and more than that, hard to hear. How to fix them was a whole other thing.

"Yes, that's it." She ran a hand down the skirt of her dress, smoothing it out in that prissy way that was so her. "Sooo, is there a special—"

Before Jada could say anything else, the front door banged open and the two boys ran in.

"Mommy?" Zack Jr. called out before he spotted Liam. "Hey, Uncle Liam!" he ran into the living room followed by Michael Jr. and they both pulled up short at the sight of Jada.

"Oh my, God! What happened to you?" she shrieked, her eyes huge and the look of horror on her face as she took in little Zack's appearance was almost comical.

The kid grinned and Liam couldn't help but chuckle under his breath.

"We were playing," Mike Jr. provided. He was a year older than Zack, who was moving toward his mom.

"Daddy, let me play football. I got a little dirty."

"A little?" Jada screeched again, keeping her distance from him. "You're...you're so..."

Zack Sr. strolled in at that moment, and Jada glared at her husband.

"He's filthy! I thought we agreed that he wasn't going to play football. He's just a baby."

"I'm not a baby."

"He's not a baby."

Zack and Jr. said in unison.

Liam burst out laughing, ignoring the daggers Jada shot him with her eyes. His sister hated dirt, especially if it was on her or her child. Heck, his nephew couldn't even get a scuff mark on his shoes without her wanting to buy him a new pair.

As for Zack, he was the opposite. He had played professional football for over ten years, becoming one of the league's best running backs before retiring. Being outdoors and getting dirty was in his DNA.

"C'mere with your fine self," Zack said, wrapping an arm around Jada's waist. He pulled her against his large frame, unfazed by her outburst. "Let me wiped that frown off of those sweet lips."

Liam shook his head. "Really, dude? You gon' kiss my sister like that in front of me?"

"Eww," the boys yelled and ran out of the room and back outside where Liam assumed Michael was.

Zack shrugged when he ended the kiss. "Can't help it, man. My woman is too sexy for me to let opportunities like that pass me by."

To his credit, the kiss must've worked because Jada had calmed down and hadn't said another word.

"I'll get lil Zack cleaned up and then we can head to dinner." Zack held Jada's hand and turned to Liam. "You sure you don't want to go out with us tonight?"

"Positive. I'm heading to Manhattan so I can start my real vacation."

His plan had been to spend a few days with his family and then the rest of the week touring the city. He had already booked a hotel and was looking forward to some alone time.

"But if one of you can drop me off at the nearest subway station, that would be good."

"We shouldn't take him anywhere since he's holding out on us," Jada said.

"Holding out about what?" Zack asked.

Liam headed to the stairs. "Nothing. Nothing at all."

*

"Here's to landing the biggest contract the company has seen so far this year." Bradley Handler clinked his tumbler of Tennessee whiskey to Charlee's glass of red wine.

They were sitting in the hotel bar, celebrating her big win. Each time Bradley got a refill of his drink, he posed a different toast. This one made number three. He seemed just as happy for her as she was for herself, and now Charlee was glad he had come along on the trip. Having him in the meeting, even if he didn't have to add much to the discussion, had been comforting.

They had arrived in New York the day before and nervous energy had her going over her presentation what seemed like a hundred times. By the time she finally drifted off to sleep, Charlee had dreamed about the impending meeting.

Now, it was all worth it. She still couldn't believe that she had convinced Edward Richardson and his team to use Fenlon exclusively for construction equipment. She'd had a lot of accomplishments over the years, but this one ranked in her top five.

Charlee took a sip from her almost empty glass, thinking about how she'd made a fool of herself. The moment they left Richardson's building, she had screamed her excitement and leaped into Bradley's arms. Well, maybe she hadn't exactly leaped, but she had definitely pounced on him, hugging him so tight that they both almost toppled over. But for the first time in a long time, she wished she had a significant other to share the news with.

When Liam and her were dating, she could call him anytime about anything. He might not have like her putting work before him, but he was always there to support and encourage her. Even times when all she wanted to do was vent. That was when his limited talking came in handy and all he did was listen.

What would he say if she called now and shared the news with him?

"Char—lee," Bradley said her name as if testing it out on his tongue. "Charlee is an interesting name. Are you named after someone?"

Charlee glanced at him and smiled. "Yeah, it's a cross between my mother and father's first name. My mother name was Charlotte."

Bradley nodded. "And when you add Kingslee you get Charlee. Clever. A beautiful name for a stunning woman." He pushed a stray curl out of her face.

The move was so intimate. A little too intimate, but she wouldn't read too much into it. They'd gotten a bit too comfortable, even flirted some over the last couple of hours. Bradley might've been feeling a little bolder considering the number of drinks he'd had.

For the most part, he was a nice guy. He'd done some harmless flirting over the years and they didn't have any issues until about six to eight months ago, after he moved to the executive floor at Fenlon. Charlee had made the mistake of going to dinner with him, and he took it as more than two executive co-workers hanging out. After he tried to kiss her, she made it clear that they could never be more than friends. Besides, she didn't date co-workers.

Tonight though…

Wait. Nope, I'm not going there.

Charlee wasn't sure if it was her sex drought or that second glass of wine, but her body yearned for some male companionship. Too bad Bradley wasn't the man she wanted. Now that she and Liam had kissed and called a truce, no other man would do.

"All right. I think it's time for me to call it a night," she said, and brought the glass of wine to her lips, taking a hefty swig.

"Your father mentioned that you were lonely."

Charlee gagged when the wine slid down her throat wrong, and she coughed, trying to clear her airway. "What?" she croaked.

Bradley stood, concern on his face and he gently patted her back. "You okay?"

She nodded and coughed again. "I'm fine. I don't know why my father told you that, but… Why were you two even discussing my personal life?"

"We weren't really, at least not initially. He asked was I dating. I told him no. Then he started talking about young people today, always putting their career before personal relationships. He mentioned you weren't dating, but that you were—"

"I like you, Bradley. You're a nice guy, but like I've told you before, I'm not interested in you that way."

Still standing, he lowered his voice. "So you've said, which is too bad. We'd be great together." When he leaned within inches of her mouth, she pushed against his chest.

Charlee moved off the bar stool. "I think we ought to call it an evening. I have a feeling you're at your limit as far as drinks."

"Wait, don't go. I'm sorry. I misjudged this evening. I thought…" he swallowed and rubbed the back of his neck, still holding a drink in his other hand. "It doesn't matter what

I thought. Since neither of us have eaten, why don't we head to the restaurant and get some dinner."

"I have plans for this evening." She really didn't, but she'd make some as soon as she got back to her room. Even if those plans only included ordering room service. "I'll see you tomorrow."

He gently grabbed hold of her elbow to keep her from walking away. "Come on. Just dinner. I'll be on my best behavior."

"Sorry, but I..." Her words stalled in her throat, and she blinked several times to figure out if she was seeing what she thought she was seeing.

Either I've had one too many glasses of wine, or one of my fantasies have come true, Charlee thought as Liam stood near the entrance to the bar. Shock and excitement warred within her as she stared in disbelief, hoping her mind wasn't playing tricks on her. Intense dark eyes. Full sexy beard. A body that looked as if he worked out twice a day, seven days a week.

Then he moved further into the space with a confident swagger.

Yep. It was him.

Her heart kicked inside her chest. He wasn't just a figment of her imagination.

Goodness. He was one sexy man in the untucked, white button-down shirt. The top three buttons were undone, showing smooth chestnut skin and his sleeves were rolled up past his wrists, muscular forearms on full display. Khakis molded over his powerful thighs and cover his long legs.

He looked so good. Too good to be strolling into a bar alone. No doubt he caught the attention of every available woman in the place.

But at the moment, he only had eyes for her.

Charlee held his gaze until his eyes narrowed and he glanced from her to Bradley, and then back at her. She pulled her arm out of Bradley's light grasp. The last thing she wanted was for Liam to get the wrong impression.

As he approached, an idea formed in her head.

The moment he was close enough, Charlee ran one of her hands up his torso. "I've been waiting for you. What took you so long?" she asked, staring into his eyes, hoping he'd play along.

Chapter Fourteen

Liam stared down into Charlee's mischievous eyes wondering what she was up to, but at the moment, he didn't care. Shocked didn't begin to express how stunned he was to see her.

"Got caught up. You missed me?" he asked in response to her question, his hand landing on her narrow waist. Clearly, he had responded correctly if her sensual smile was any indication. Her hands inched up his chest, and she looped her arms around his neck, bringing her face close to his.

"I've missed you more than you know," she whispered, then surprised the hell out of him when her soft, red lips covered his. The kiss was slow, thoughtful, and oh so damn sweet. She caught him on the wrong day if she thought she could kiss him like this and not get something started.

His self-control and common sense when it came to her was shot, gone, non-existent. The days of fighting his feelings—over. After being around lovey-dovey couples for all of his life and even more so the last few days, he was reminded that they'd all taken a chance on love. They had opened themselves up to potential heartbreak to be with the one they loved.

Liam had another chance, and he planned to take it.

He was tired of fighting his feelings for Charlee, and had intended to let her know how he felt once he returned to Cincinnati. Little did he know that he'd run into the source of his unsettled thoughts and sleepless nights.

He tightened his hold on her, deepening the kiss as their tongues tangled to a familiar beat. He missed her more than he cared to admit. Not just since he'd seen her the week before, he craved everything they once shared, including her hypnotic kisses.

When he walked in and saw her sitting at the bar, he thought his eyes were playing tricks on him. It took him a few minutes to realize that it was really her. In New York. At his hotel. Only a few feet from him. What he didn't know was why she was there.

Again, at the moment, it didn't matter. This was a helleva way to say hello.

Someone nearby cleared their throat, reminding Liam where they were. He slowly lifted his head. "Maybe we can finish that a little later," he said to Charlee. Normally, he wasn't big on public displays of affection. Yet, when it came to her, he rarely acted like himself. Why should this instance be any different?

"We can definitely do that." Charlee ran her finger over his bottom lip just as he started to swipe his tongue across it. They both smiled, and she proceeded to wipe lipstick from his mouth.

Once she was finished, Liam thanked her and reluctantly pulled his gaze from hers and finally took a good look at the man she'd been with. With a glass of liquor in his hand, the guy studied him, probably thinking the same thing as Liam. He seemed familiar. While they were close in height and build, he appeared to be a few years older than Liam who had recently turned thirty-two.

"Let me introduce you to my co-worker." Charlee repositioned herself, looping her arm through Liam's, holding on tight as if afraid he'd move away. "This is Bradley Handler, one of the executives at Fenlon."

116

So that's why the guy looked familiar. Liam must have seen him at their office at some point.

"Bradley and I met with a client earlier and decided to have a celebratory drink. Oh, and Bradley, this is Liam Jenkins."

Liam shook his hand before returning his attention to Charlee. "So, what are you celebrating?"

Her eyes sparkled with excitement. "I just—"

"This amazing woman just closed a huge deal for Fenlon," Bradley spoke over Charlee, looking at her like a proud lover. "Those guys didn't stand a chance. Beauty and brains. A lethal combination."

Liam ignored the sudden bout of jealousy creeping through him and smiled down at Charlee who was looking at him shyly. That expression was new. The woman didn't have a shy bone in her body.

"Congratulations, sweetheart." He tipped her chin up with the pad of his finger and brushed his lips over hers, taking full advantage of their charade that felt real to him. Liam didn't have to look at her co-worker. The heat from Bradley's stare burned through him. "We should head out and do some celebrating. I can't wait to hear the details."

Again, he must've said the right thing if Charlee's full-blown grin was any indication.

"I guess these were the plans you were talking about," Bradley said dryly to Charlee, finishing off his drink before plunking the empty glass onto the bar. "Are you guys...together?"

"Yes," Liam and Charlee said in unison.

Liam eased out of her hold and wrapped his arm around her waist, a wave of possessiveness engulfing him. Though they hadn't actually talked about a reconciliation, he knew their feelings were in sync. No way could she kiss him the way she had if there wasn't something between them.

"Thanks for keeping my lady company. I can take it from here."

Bradley buttoned his suit jacket, his gaze steady on Charlee as he nodded. "Apparently, you're not as lonely as your father made you out to be."

Charlee stiffened against Liam. "You know what, Bradley? I don't appreciate the two of you discussing me...about *anything*. My father doesn't know everything about me. I'll be sure to let him know that too when I see him. As for you, I'm *still* not interested."

"Have a good night, Bradley," Liam said. "I know we will."

*

Charlee was glad Liam led her out of the bar. Otherwise, she might have hauled off and smacked that smug look off of Bradley's face. He could've kept his last comment to himself instead of acting like an ass and attempting to embarrass her.

So much for trying to let him down easy. Had she known their friendly banter or flirtatious comments would lead to him showing his true self, she would've skipped the celebratory drinks. And how dare her father discuss her personal life with anybody, especially some guy she worked with. He was definitely going to hear from her. She might call tonight to set him straight instead of waiting until she returned to Cincinnati. Even if she had been lonely lately, that was nobody's business but hers.

"You care to tell me what all of that was about back there?" Liam slowed down once they got outside. The covered area in front of the hotel where guests were catching taxis and looking for their Uber drivers was more crowded than it had been earlier.

Liam tugged on her hand. "Let's step over here."

They moved a distance away from the entrance. He stood in front of her, his wide shoulders blocking her view of all the activity going on around them. It was as if he was shielding her while she got her emotions under control.

Charlee didn't speak right away, feeling a little foolish for using him to get away from Bradley.

The jerk.

She released a sigh, more frustrated with herself than Bradley. She couldn't be mad at him, at least not totally. It was her fault she chose to give him any of her time, confusing their relationship by being too friendly. More than anything, she was angry that he and her father had discussions about her. It was bad enough her dad somehow knew she'd been a little lonely lately, but how could he betray her by saying something to Bradley?

Liam squeezed her hand. "Talk to me."

She hesitated, but then said. "Thank you for what you did back there. I appreciate you playing along."

"Why did you need me to *play along*?"

"Bradley was getting a little...friendly, trying to talk me into going to dinner with him. I tried letting him down nicely, not wanting things to be weird when we return to the office. Now that I know he and my father have been talking about me behind my back, I'm done with nice. I am so pissed at my dad. How could he tell some guy I work with that I'm lonely?" she choked out, humiliation clogging her throat.

She didn't embarrass easily, but her personal life was a sensitive subject. It was the one area that she didn't have a good grasp on and kept getting wrong. Ask her anything about construction equipment, business finance, or how to manage a large staff, and she could tell you anything you needed to know. Ask her about her favorite hobby, the latest R & B songs, or how to keep a man, and she wouldn't have an answer.

"Why would Kingslee assume something like that? You're the most energetic, fun-loving, outgoing person I know. I wouldn't be surprised if men were banging on your door for a chance to go out with you. So how exactly did your father come to this conclusion? *Are* you lonely?"

Charlee swallowed the sob that was creeping up her throat and lowered her gaze. No one wanted to admit that outside of their job, they didn't have much of a life. There had been a time when she'd been alone, but hadn't felt lonely. Lately, though, something had been missing in her life. Her career wasn't as fulfilling as it used to be which was one of the reasons why she wanted the CEO position. She hoped that the new challenges would fill the void.

"Look at me," Liam said.

Charlee met his gaze and wasn't sure exactly what he saw in her eyes, but without a word, he gathered her into his strong arms. He placed a kiss against her temple and held her without saying a word.

Charlee soaked up the comfort he provided, but she didn't want his pity. She loved him, would always love him. Yet, she wanted him to see her like he used to. Like the confident, courageous, outgoing woman he had once fallen in love with. The woman she was when they were a couple.

With one last squeeze, he slowly released her and folded his arms across his broad chest. Let's get back to Bradley. You were using me to get a rise out of the guy, huh?"

Charlee's heart sank. That might've been her intention, but not the way he made it sound. "Liam, I would never use you li—"

"Hey," he cupped her cheek, his dark gaze staring into her eyes, "I'm not complaining. I enjoyed every minute of our ruse. Feel free to use me like that anytime."

Her world teetered. Was he saying what she thought he was saying? He enjoyed their lip-locking? Pretending they were a couple?

Now that Charlee thought about it, when Bradley asked if they were together, she and Liam both said, yes. She wanted nothing more than a second chance with him, but before a few minutes ago, it was clear he hadn't been ready for that. Now? She could only hope.

Something had changed. She had a feeling it happened before he stepped into the bar. Liam didn't play games. If he wasn't interested in more than a friendship, he wouldn't have returned her kiss. He also wouldn't have said they were together.

Then again, he might've done it to help her save face.

"Are you hungry?" he asked, as if his words from a moment ago hadn't just thrown her off-kilter.

Charlee didn't want to get her hopes up, and she definitely didn't want to question what he'd said about using him anytime. Not yet at least. Liam was a complex man, but always a straight shooter. She'd know soon enough what was going on in his head.

"I'm starving," she finally said.

"Me too, and over dinner you can tell me about this deal you closed on. Now, what would you like to eat?"

Charlee gave a slight shrug, not caring where they went as long as she ate and they were together. "It doesn't matter. You know what I like."

"Yeah, I know what you like, but what would you like to eat?"

She stared at him in surprise then burst out laughing and couldn't stop, especially when he frowned at her.

"When did you start cracking jokes?" She dabbed at the corner of her eyes with the palm of her hand. "And *who are you*? What have you done with *my* Liam? You know, the one who gives one-word answers, rarely flirts, and only cracks a smile when I'm around."

"Would you believe me if I said I've changed?"

"Uhh...*no*."

The corner of his lips quirked. "Okay, fair enough. I guess I'll have to show you that I'm not the same man."

He looked her over. His gaze taking in her pink, sleeveless blouse, gray skirt that stopped just above her knees, and the tall gray pumps on her feet. She had folded the short jacket of her suit and put it in her bag that was hanging from her shoulder.

"Do you need to change shoes? I was thinking about us walking a few blocks."

"I'll be fine." She hadn't changed after the meeting and usually wore heels all day long.

"So you're okay if we don't eat here?" He gestured toward the door of the hotel.

"I'll be happy to go anywhere you go," she said honestly. She wanted to take her mind off of work, her father, Cincinnati and anything else that wasn't a part of her right-here-and-right-now moment.

"All right, then let's get out of here."

They started walking, but Charlee stopped abruptly. "Wait. I didn't get a chance to ask. What are you doing in New York and at my hotel?"

"Actually, this is my hotel, too. I was visiting family in Brooklyn for the last few days and figured I'd spend the rest of my mini-vacation in Manhattan."

"Fate," Charlee said in awe, excitement doing a jig inside of her body. "That's what this is, fate. We were destined to run into each other."

"If you say so." He started guiding them toward West 46th street where Charlee could already see the swarm of people covering the sidewalks. She loved New York and its energy, but right now, she wished that she could have Liam all to herself. No people. No crowds. Nothing. Nothing but them together hanging out in Times Square.

Chapter Fifteen

A short while later, they found a twenty-four-hour diner and had already placed their order. It was no wonder Charlee had been hungry. It was after nine, and she'd been in the bar longer than she realized.

She glanced around the cozy space where practically every table was occupied. Almost everyone was eating. Maybe that meant that they wouldn't have to wait long for their food.

Her gaze landed on Liam, sitting on the other side of the high-back booth. It seemed surreal that she was actually there with him...in New York...about to have dinner. She couldn't have planned the way the evening had shaped up even if she tried.

"What? Why are you staring at me?" Liam asked, lifting the steaming cup of coffee to his mouth.

"It always amazes me that you can drink coffee all day long and it not keep you awake at night."

He shrugged. "I'm immune to the caffeine, but I enjoy the taste...usually." He frowned after taking a sip.

"Is it that bad?"

"Worse." He slid the mug to the end of the table. "Let's hope the food is better."

"All right, here we go," their server said, holding a large, round tray. "I have French toast stuffed with bananas, Nutella and graham crackers with a side of bacon for you." She set the plate of food in front of Charlee.

Everything looked delicious, and she couldn't wait to dive in. She only wished she had thought to order hash browns, knowing Liam wouldn't share his.

"And for you," the server continued, setting dishes in front of Liam, "we have a Spanish omelet with onions, peppers, and salsa roja with a side of hash browns and sausage links." She lowered the tray to her side. "Can I get either of you anything else?"

"Not for me," Charlee said, and looked at Liam.

"How about a couple of waters? Also, can you bring her more hot water and a side of hash browns?"

This man, Charlee thought. She had a weakness for practically anything made out of potatoes and tried to keep her consumption to a minimum. For her, they were like desserts. Once she had a taste, she couldn't stop eating them.

"I'll be right back with those items," the server said before leaving the table.

Charlee twisted her mouth and narrowed her eyes at Liam, trying to look offended. The smirk on his face basically said that she was failing miserably.

"Are you afraid that I'm going to ask for some of your hash browns?"

"I *know* you are. Since I don't want to have to stab you with my fork when you try to take them, I figured we should just get your own."

"You think you know me, huh?"

"Yup. I probably know you better than anyone."

Charlee nodded slowly in agreement. There had been times when she thought he knew her better than she knew herself. Too often he had predicted a need or his thoughtfulness got her exactly what she needed on occasion.

Yeah, he knew her well.

They dug in and she tried not to moan her pleasure. The coffee had to be horrid for Liam not to drink it, but the food was terrific. Neither of them spoke for the first five or ten minutes of eating.

"We'll have to come back here sometime. This is good. How's yours?" he asked.

Charlee hesitated in responding, stuck on the part where he said—we'll have to come back here sometime. Now she really needed to know what his intentions were. She wasn't the most patient person and wanted to push for answers, but she'd wait and follow his lead for the moment. Even if it killed her.

"Charlee?" He frowned as he stared across the table at her, his fork mid-air. "What's wrong? You don't like the food?"

She shook her head. "Uh, no. I—I mean, it's good. Very good. Maybe you should try again with the coffee. That might've just been a bad batch."

"Nah. We can stop somewhere else after we leave here. So, tell me about your presentation."

For the next few minutes, she recapped her presentation, getting excited about the deal all over again. The idea had been her brainchild and something they hadn't offered any other clients until now. Since the Richardson Group had been buying equipment and tools from them for years, they were the perfect company to start with. The goal was to convince them to use Fenlon's equipment exclusively.

Once she had finished presenting, the group, four men of various nationalities in their late fifties, early sixties, directed their questions to Bradley. Charlee didn't take offense or allow them to overlook her. She made it clear that she was the one with the answers. If they wondered why Bradley was there, they didn't ask.

"I made them an offer that they would've been fools to pass up. They just had to agree to use our equipment exclusively for a specified amount of time." Charlee shrugged. "And before I knew it, the CEO asked—where do I sign?"

Liam nodded, the huge smile on his face enhancing her excitement. "I'm proud of you, but I'm not surprised. You're creative, and your innovative ideas have been helping your father's company for years. This is just another example of that. There will be more huge contracts to come, thanks to you."

Charlee's cheeks heated. She couldn't stop the grin that spread across her face. Liam's words meant everything. He was a perfectionist. His architectural skills—second to none. Hearing him give her such positive accolades was almost as thrilling as landing the contract. He also knew how important it was for her to succeed in her career.

"What was the purpose of having Bradley along if this was your project?"

"Don't get me started, but my father thought the presentation would go better if Bradley was present since this group was used to dealing with men in this industry. I proved that a woman can do the same job if not better."

Liam nodded as he finished off his omelet. "That you did."

"I'll admit, I was a little salty about my father's decision. I've always traveled and done my presentations solo, and I did them successfully. I can't help but wonder if something else was behind his decision."

She and Bradley were equals as far as their positions in the company. Maybe sending him on the trip was part of her father grooming the man for the CEO job. The more he knew about the clients, especially clients that had been with the company since the beginning, the better Bradley would know how to deal with them in the future.

"Are you still traveling a lot?" Liam asked, the serious expression that she was used to seeing was back, his tone solemn.

The evening was going great, and the last thing she wanted was for her traveling schedule to overshadow their time together. Memories of their past problems came rushing back.

"I occasionally travel for work, but not nearly as much as I used to," she said honestly. "When I became a part of the senior management team, I inherited support staff who does more traveling than I do."

His expression didn't change. The thrill that Charlee felt earlier about the possibility of a reconciliation waned. Who was she kidding? Liam was who he was, and she respected the fact that he knew what he wanted and what he didn't. The difference now was that she wanted what he wanted. More importantly, she wanted him.

"I want you back," she blurted.

So much for patience.

Charlee braced herself for whatever he'd say next. If he didn't say the right thing, she'd move on and wouldn't look back. She had never been shy about going after what she wanted or asking for what she needed. Except with Liam. He had the ability to hurt her feelings with a simple no. And receiving a no from him would be a thousand times worse than from anyone else.

Holding his gaze, she dared him to tell her that he didn't want the same thing. Before their ruse at the bar, she hadn't been positive that she'd get a second chance with him. Sure, the last few times they'd kiss were like old times, but his words the other morning at his house had given her pause. But the vibe she'd gotten off of him at the bar was giving her renewed hope.

"How long are you in town for?" he asked, not bothering to comment on her declaration.

"I was planning to leave tomorrow unless you give me a reason to stay."

Seconds ticked by as he searched her eyes. Then he looked away. Not before Charlee saw a barely-there smile play around his lips and a slight shake of his head.

He wanted her back.

He didn't have to say it. She knew it down deep in her soul. Hope blossomed inside her chest at the realization.

If you want something bad enough, don't be afraid to go after it.

Her father's words rang through her mind, giving her a renewed energy. There wasn't anything she wanted more than Liam. Not even the CEO position at Fenlon or the pair of red Jimmy Choos she'd been drooling over a few weeks ago.

"How long are you planning to stay in New York?" she asked.

"I'll be here four more days."

Charlee waited, hoping he'd say more. When he didn't, she asked, "Are you going to—"

"What would it take for you to spend the next four days with me?"

In spite of the butterflies bouncing around inside of her belly, Charlee played it cool. "Ask me to stay."

After a slight hesitation, Liam slid out of the booth and sat next to her, one arm draped the back of the seat behind her. An intense shiver of wanting rushed through her body as the clean, fresh scent of his cologne washed over her like a hypnotic drug.

His nearness was overwhelming. All she could do was sit there watching him in stunned silence.

Gently grasping her hand, he slowly turned it over and placed a feathery kiss on the inside of her wrist, and then another on her forearm. He slowly worked his way up and his soft lips on her heated skin was like a healing balm to her soul. He didn't stop the sweet torture until he reached the bend of her arm.

Her heart nearly pounded out of her chest at the tingling sensation that shot to the tips of her toes. It had nothing to do with her pointy shoes being a little snug, but everything to do with his mouth on her body. The sultry hunger in his eyes and his potent magnetism had her pulse skittering out of control.

Dang. His seduction skills were still on point.

Still holding her hand, he unhurriedly brought the back of her fingers to his lips, his gaze steady on hers.

"Stay with me," he crooned.

Charlee nodded, unable to get her mouth to work to release the words that were screaming in her mind. Hell, yeah, she'd stay with him. If given the chance, she would spend the rest of her life with this sweet, complicated man.

For now, she'd settle for spending four glorious days with him and hope that they'd turn into more.

Chapter Sixteen

"You will never believe who's in New York," Charlee said the moment Rayne answered her work phone.

"Is that a trick question? You told me last week that you were going. Something about a meeting that was a big deal."

"Yeah, I know, but guess who I ran into last night?"

Charlee sat in the upholstered chair in her hotel room and fastened the thin straps of her sandals. She had only brought two extra outfits with her to New York and looked forward to doing a little shopping.

A smile broke free at the thought of getting Liam to go shopping with her. She could already hear him groaning about bouncing from one store to another.

Stay with me.

Those three little words from him had made her evening, and of course she accepted. Even if she'd had back to back meetings scheduled all four days, she would've canceled every single one to be with him.

"Girl, how should I know? It could be anyone. Just tell me."

"Liam."

A moment ago, Charlee had heard paper rustling over the phone line. Now there was only silence. She pulled the phone away from her ear to see if the call had dropped, but Rayne's name was still on the screen.

"Hello? Are you still there?" she asked.

"Yeah, I'm still here. I'm just trying to wrap my brain around the fact that you ran into Liam of all people. *How* did that happen? Did you know he'd be there?"

"No, I didn't."

She told her friend everything, starting with the scene at the bar. After dinner, she and Liam had gone to a coffee shop so that he could get his fix. Then they took a ferry from Manhattan to Staten Island and back. It had been a dreamy evening. Clear skies, a gentle breeze, and being wrapped in Liam's arms was the perfect way to end an evening. It felt as if they hadn't been apart.

She had been anxious when he walked her to her hotel room. She wanted so bad for him to spend the night, even if they just held each other. He told her his willpower to keep his hands to himself was shot and he kissed her at the door, bid her a good night, and promised to see her in the morning.

"Oh. My. Goodness! I knew he was still in love because of the way he always looks at you, but what changed?" Rayne asked, excitement ringing in her voice.

"Girl, I'm not sure." She told her about the day at his house, as well as the text messages.

"This is it. He wants you back. He's just too much of a *guy* to make it clear. But still, I can't believe he asked you to stay!"

"I know, right?"

"This is the second chance you've been waiting for."

Charlee agreed. She had no intention of being her usual pushy self. This was the perfect opportunity for them to get reacquainted and find their way back to each other for good.

"I already know you guys are going to have a good time on this mini-vacation, especially if last night was any indication. Just be careful and don't do anything crazy, like skinny dipping in the Hudson River or parachuting off the Empire State building."

"Now, would I do anything that dangerous?"

"Yes!"

They both laughed, knowing she would try almost anything once.

"When you get back home, I want all the details."

"Definitely," Charlee said, then heard someone at the door. "Hey, I gotta go. Wish me luck."

"Good luck!"

She disconnected the call and tossed her cell phone onto the bed on the way to the door. Looking through the peephole, she released a relieved breath, glad it wasn't Liam since she hadn't done her hair yet.

She swung the door open. "Hey there. Did you get my message?" She had called Bradley the night before, after returning from dinner, to let him know that she wasn't flying out with him.

"No, what message?" His appreciative gaze traveled slowly down her body and back up again, taking in her red halter dress and matching sandals. "You look great, but aren't you going to be a little cold on the plane?"

"That's the message I left on your voicemail. I'm staying in New York a few days. I already alerted the staff and wanted to let you know, too."

"Oh, okay," Bradley said slowly, disappointment in his tone. "I guess you'll be spending that time with the guy from last night, huh?"

"Yes," she said without elaborating.

Bradley glanced down at the rolling suitcase at his side before returning his attention to her. "I owe you an apology. I was out of order last night. We were having a good time and I guess I took that as a sign that you were into me as much as I'm into you."

"No apology needed. Nothing happened. We were both excited about the presentation and after a couple of drinks..." She shrugged. "No harm done."

Charlee meant it when she told him no apology necessary. After spending the evening with Liam, it dawned on her that she might not have known he was in New York had she not been in the bar with Bradley. She also had time to think about their professional relationship. They had to be able to work together without any awkwardness. She didn't want either of them to ever misunderstand the other's intentions again. What might've started as an innocent interaction could have easily turn into a situation that they both would've regretted if it had gone too far.

"So we're cool?" he asked carefully, his dark, bushy brows lifted skyward.

"We're cool." Charlee still planned to have a long talk with her father. "You have a safe trip, and I'll see you in a few days."

After they said their goodbyes, she returned to the bathroom to try and do something with her hair. The forecast called for sunshine and eighty-degrees, so leaving her curls down was out of the question.

She gathered the long strands into a ponytail on top of her head, keeping a few curly tendrils loose around her face. After a few more minutes of primping, adding silver, hoop earrings, a necklace and a few bangles, she was satisfied with the way she looked. She left the bathroom and rushed around the room, tidying up some just in case Liam came in. If by chance the day went the way she was planning, he'd be returning to the room with her.

A quick knock sounded at the door, and she blew out a nervous breath as she went to open it.

Here goes.

She had to make this second chance count.

*

Liam stood dumbfounded. All types of impure thoughts raced through his mind as he gave Charlee a once over, and then another, but slower this time.

How is it that she got more beautiful each time he saw her? It just didn't make sense. He had always loved her full, mane of red curls, especially when piled on top of her head like they were now. The loose ponytail gave him an unobstructed view of her graceful neck. Not only that. The long, curly tendrils that framed her face brought attention to her big, pretty eyes. She never wore much makeup, but today she had on eyeshadow that brought out the gold specks in her brown orbs.

And that body.

Lord, that body.

The sundress had a deep V in the front. Low enough to show that she was well endowed with nice, full breasts, but not low enough to be inappropriate. It had two straps that tied behind her neck. The outfit was snug over her slim, but curvy body and stopped just above her knees.

The whole package had him tempted to push her back into the room to start their day with love-making instead of sightseeing. It had taken a herculean effort to leave her at the door last night and not take her up on the invitation to spend the night. He wanted her too bad.

"Hellooo?" Charlee waved her hand in front of his face, giving him a whiff of her subtle lavender and vanilla fragrance. "What's wrong with you?"

Seriously? She really just asked him that?

"You." His voice hitched, and he cleared his throat. "Maybe we should stay in, and I refamiliarize myself with your magnificent body." There he went again, speaking before his brain was engaged. The words tumbled out of Liam's mouth before he could snatch them back.

Charlee's brows inched up. "Umm…okay," she said slowly and stepped back, opening the door wider, but Liam didn't move. He wanted her like he wanted no other woman, and not just her body. He wanted all of her. Mind, body, and soul. Jumping in bed before they were *officially* back together wouldn't be a good idea.

"Grab your stuff and let's go," Liam said gruffly, coming back to his senses. He had to keep his head over the next four days with this exquisite temptress.

She pursed her lips and frowned. "Liam...so help me I'm going to hurt you. You can't be getting a girl's hopes all up and then change your mind."

He couldn't help but laugh at her mock disappointment and the exaggerated way she grabbed a small purse from a table and walked out.

"Should I be worried? You're acting like...like not yourself. What happened to you?"

She gasped when he backed her into a nearby wall.

"You're what's happened to me. I told you. You make me crazy, woman. I don't even recognize myself half the time whenever you're anywhere near me."

A seductive smile graced her glossy lips, and she cupped his face between her hands. "I missed you...and your beard." Her fingers grazed over the hair on his cheeks. "*Oh*, and I feel the same way about you, except I'm not as crazy." She gave a small laugh that got smothered when Liam covered her mouth with his.

It was dangerous to kiss her when he felt so out of control, but he had to taste her again. With one hand on her hip and the other cradling the back of her head, he moved his mouth over hers, devouring its softness. As usual, she felt perfect in his arms. He had been a fool thinking that he could live without her. This woman was a part of him. She owned his heart.

Their tongues dueled, and Charlee kissed him with a hunger that matched his, only making his need for her that much more intense. They should stop, but...not yet. And when she slid her arms over his shoulders and around his neck, Liam knew if they didn't stop soon, they'd never get out to experience the city together.

"Get a room," somebody murmured in passing before girls burst out into giggles.

With one last kiss, Liam slowly lifted his head but didn't release Charlee right away. He wanted to hold her just a little longer.

"I guess that means that you're happy to see me, huh?"

He brushed his thumb over her cheek. "I'm more than happy to see you. I haven't been able to stop thinking about you." Her eyes softened and he gave her another quick peck. "Ready to get going?"

"Yes, and after breakfast, I was thinking we could go shopping."

Liam dropped his arms from around her and groaned. "I can't believe you're going to torture me with shopping on our first day together."

She slipped her arm through his and pulled him toward the elevators. "Don't look at it as torture. Look at it as a chance to see me in some super-cute outfits. I'll even let you pick one. Maybe even some lingerie."

Liam perked up. A lingerie store could be dangerous to his psyche, but hell, he was on vacation. "All right, and since we're in New York, I'll go with the flow. I'm going to live a little, take a walk on the wild side."

Charlee stopped abruptly. "*Really? You?*"

"For real. Whatever you want to do over the next few days, I'm game."

She considered him for a minute, not looking too convinced and probably trying to determine if he was serious. Eventually, a smile spread across her tempting mouth.

"So, anything I want to do, you'll go along with it?"

He narrowed his eyes. This woman had a wild streak, and God only knew what she'd have him doing, but hey, what was the worst that could happen?

"Anything," he said with more bravado than he felt. Yet, there was a part of him that couldn't wait to see what they got into.

They entered the elevator and Liam nodded at a guy that was already on there. Once they started moving, the car seemed to stop on every floor with people getting on with luggage. Before long, Charlee was squished against him. He didn't mind, deciding to take full advantage of her nearness.

He wrapped his arms around her from behind, his hand resting on her flat stomach as he nuzzled her scented neck.

She felt fantastic against him. He couldn't keep his hands or mouth off of her, especially when she snuggled closer.

"I'm glad you were able to stay," he whispered in her ear. "And I want you back."

She jerked her head to look at him over her shoulder and banged into his chin.

"Ow," he said under his breath, rubbing the offended area as she stared at him wide-eyed. He probably could've waited until they were alone, but he just needed to get it out. He also probably could've come up with a better way to let her know that he wanted her back in his life.

Seriously? she mouthed.

The elevator stopped again but was too crowded for anyone else to get on.

Liam nodded, and she cupped his cheek, her thumb skimming over his beard, something she used to do often. He placed a kiss on her forehead just as they reached the ground floor.

"I want that too," Charlee said the moment they were off the elevator. "I know we still have things to work through, but there's nothing I want more than for us to be back together."

"Me too. We'll take our time. Get to know each other again and see what happens."

Grinning, she kissed him. "We're going to have so much fun!"

Her excitement was palpable. It had been a long time since Liam looked forward to anything, and with Charlee he was all in. He planned to do whatever it took to have her in his life for good.

Hand in hand, they headed to the main exit until she pulled up short.

"Oh crap. We can't leave yet. I forgot to call and extend my stay. Give me a minute. I need to stop at the front desk to add a few days onto my reservation."

They both walked over and only stood in line a short while until the next front desk associate was available.

"Good morning, are you checking out?"

"No, actually, I'd like to extend my stay." Charlee gave the woman the dates and they waited while she checked her computer.

"I'm sorry, Ms. Fenlon. We're completely full for tonight, but we have rooms available for the other two nights."

Charlee's shoulders sagged. "Are you sure? Can you check again?"

"Actually," Liam leaned against the counter. "That won't be necessary. She can stay with me."

"Liam, you don't have—"

"Anything goes, remember?"

After a short hesitation, a playful gleam radiated in her eyes. "Oh, I remember. You just make sure you don't forget."

Chapter Seventeen

"I don't know about this, Charlee."

Liam had said those words several times in different ways from the moment she first mentioned the crazy idea on their way downtown. Now that they were walking toward the East River Pier, he was having second thoughts. It wasn't that he was afraid of heights, but the possibility of falling out of the sky did give him pause. Besides, taking a helicopter ride had never been on his list of things to do.

"Come on, Liam. Where's your sense of adventure? Anyway, the tour is only twenty minutes. It'll be over before we know it, and it'll be fun."

"All right," he said slowly. "If you say so." Next time he'd be slow to agree to go along with whatever she wanted.

Forty-five minutes later, they were on the large bird with one other couple and their daughter, preparing to lift off. The rumbling rhythm of the engine and the blades, a cross between an old washing machine and a jet plane, was drowned out considerably once they put on their headsets. Adrenaline pumped through Liam's veins and his heartbeat doubled. Suddenly he couldn't wait to get a bird's-eye view of the city.

Charlee was sitting next to him, gripping his hand as if it was a lifeline as they lifted off. Her gaze was non-blinking while she stared out the window. Liam gave her a little shake, wanting to make sure she was all right. Considering how excited his little adventurer had been before climbing aboard, she hadn't said much.

The helicopter veered right and she stiffened, squeezing his hand harder.

"You okay?" he asked into the mouthpiece connected to the headset. She didn't respond, only offered a slight smile that didn't reach her eyes.

Liam shook his head and chuckled. So much for this being fun. She looked scared to death.

He glanced out the window over the water, amazement filling him as he took in Manhattan while the pilot narrated the tour. They flew over the Brooklyn and Manhattan bridges, and the slight bit of turbulence didn't detract from the unobstructed view they had of the city.

"This is absolutely breathtaking," Charlee mumbled.

Liam had to agree. In all of his years, taking a helicopter ride never crossed his mind. Now he could totally see himself doing it again.

His jaw dropped open as they approached the Statue of Liberty, never imagining that he'd ever see Lady Liberty eye to eye. "Okay. Now this is cool." Astonished by the sheer size of the monument, he took it in as if he hadn't already seen the statue on more than one occasion. There was just something about seeing it face to face that made it that much more spectacular.

By the end of the tour, they had also seen Ellis and Governor's Island, as well as the Wall Street Financial Center that he and Charlee had already visited that morning.

"I have to admit, that was one of your better suggestions," Liam said after the tour as they were leaving Pier 6. "I never would have come up with that."

"I'm glad you enjoyed yourself, but I'm glad we're back on the ground. That's it for me and helicopter rides." Charlee laughed shakily, not seeming too steady on her feet.

Holding her hand, Liam stepped off to the side and leaned against a brick building. He pulled her into the circle of his arms and held her snugly against him.

She had only spoken a few words on the tour and now was looking a little worn out. That could've been from the ride or from all that they'd done earlier. After moving her belongings to his hotel room, they had breakfast, then went for a stroll through Rockefeller Center. What was supposed to be a quick stop there had turned into a two-hour adventure. After about ten stores, Liam had been ready to put his feet up and call it a day, but he didn't complain. He was just happy to be with her.

"Are you feeling all right?"

Charlee stared up at him, her chin resting on his chest and a soft smile on her lips. "I'm fine. Maybe a little hungry, though."

"I guess I should feed you then, but first…" He let his words trail off as he lowered his head to claim her irresistible mouth.

Throughout the morning and much of the afternoon, he took every opportunity to kiss her. Now that they were back together, he couldn't get enough. He held the back of her head gently, but firm as he deepened the kiss. Each time their lips touched, he wanted her to feel what he felt deep in his soul for her.

"Mmm, that was nice," Charlee crooned when the kiss ended.

"It was, and I can't wait to do it again. How about we get you a little snack to hold you over for an hour."

"Okay, but why just a snack?"

"Because I took the liberty of making plans for an early dinner for us. We need to pick up a few items in about an hour."

"I've been with you since early this morning. When'd you have time to do that?"

"Somewhere between the tenth or twentieth outfit you tried on."

Charlee laughed and pulled away, swatting his arm in the process. "I wasn't that bad. Anyway, what's for dinner?" She slid her hand back into his, and they started walking again.

Liam glanced down at her. "How about a picnic in Central Park?"

The sweet smile that spread across her luscious lips had his heart beating faster. All the feelings from the past, the times when all he wanted to do was make her happy came rushing back. He planned to do whatever necessary to make sure this second chance got them both what they wanted.

"A picnic in the park," she said wistfully. "That sounds wonderful."

*

Charlee leaned back against Liam's hard body, amazed at how he had managed to find the perfect spot in Central Park for a picnic. Their location overlooked the Cherry Hill fountain as well as the lake. Even the mild evening temperature had cooperated. As she looked around the park near them, it was clear that her man hadn't been the only one to think of a picnic. Though it wasn't overly crowded, there were other couples and groups of people lounging nearby.

"These are great," Liam said, holding a chocolate strawberry near her mouth. "Try it."

Turning slightly, Charlee's hair brushed against his chest. She opened for him, loving the way he'd been feeding her for much of the evening.

"Mmm. You're right. That's amazing. More please."

She could feel the rumble of his chuckle against her back. She couldn't have asked for a better surprised dinner. The bite-size sandwiches, a small cheese platter, a vegetable tray, chocolate covered strawberries, and an assortment of cookies. All had been more than enough for the two of them. Even the music selection from Liam's cell phone was on point. Normally, he preferred jazz but had opted for R & B, her favorite genre.

All in all, it was the perfect evening and brought back memories of why she'd fallen in love with Liam in the first place. His thoughtfulness and resourcefulness were only a few of the qualities he possessed. Besides those, he knew her so well, what she liked and didn't like, and she loved how he predicted her needs.

"I forgot how romantic you could be." She wiped her mouth before taking a big swig from the water bottle. "What made you think of a picnic, and how'd you pull this all together?"

A shiver ran through her body when he placed a lingering kiss near her ear.

"I called the concierge at the hotel and asked if he knew of a place that catered picnics for two. He gave me a short list of possibilities. The first two places I called couldn't squeeze us in today. I ended up contacting a personal assistant who took on last-minute assignments."

"Had she done something like this before?"

"I'm not sure, but she came through and on time. She got everything I requested and had even thought to throw in insect repellent."

"In which I'm grateful."

Charlee ran her hand over the extra thick blanket. Liam and the woman had thought of everything, including plastic champagne glasses. Since it was technically illegal to drink alcohol in the park, he had opted for lemonade. They toasted to getting back together, and Charlee felt hopeful that they…that she could get it right this time. Deciding to stay in New York with Liam for a few days had been one of the best decisions she'd made in a long time. Spending the day with him still felt like a dream, a dream she never wanted to wake up from.

Charlee twisted around as graceful as she could in her sundress, her legs laying across one of Liam's.

"Thank you for doing this."

He covered her mouth with his and kissed her slowly, sending need rushing through her veins. If she had the ability to freeze time, she'd freeze it at that moment and bask in the sweetness that was Liam.

"It's my pleasure. I love doing things for you," he said when the kiss ended.

They'd been out there for the past hour and a half and the sun was starting to make its descent behind the trees. The picnic really was the perfect end to their busy tour day. With their shoes kicked off, they continued to lounge, discussing Liam's work and some of the new projects he had taken on. In order to keep up with the demands of all the work that was coming his way, he was considering going into business with another well-known architect whose work he respected.

Liam stared down into her face, caressing her cheek. After a lengthy silence, he asked, "What does it mean to you for us to be back together? What will that look like?"

Charlee hesitated, her pulse pounding fast while she searched her mind to find the right words to express what she was feeling. "I want forever with you." She lowered her eyes, struggling to say more, knowing it would make her even more vulnerable to him. "I'm not gonna lie. The last couple of years without you have been lonely. I knew I would miss you, but I didn't realize that guilt would eat at me the way it did."

He lifted her chin, forcing her to look at him. "I'm sorry, Sweetheart, for the part I played in our breakup. I should've been the one to fight harder to keep us together."

Throughout the day, they both agreed that they should have communicated better and made the necessary adjustments in their relationship.

"Since then, I've been trying to fill a void in my life. That's been mainly done by working long hours, but I realized a while ago that my career is not enough to keep me happy. It's you that I need. It's you that I want, Liam."

He lowered his head and kissed her again. "It's you that I want, too," he mumbled against her mouth. "Only you."

The music on his phone changed to an old slow jam by Luther Vandross, and Liam turned it up.

"Dance with me."

Charlee's brows shot up, and she glanced around. "Here?"

"Yeah. Why not here?" He stood and extended his hand to her, gently tugging her up. "You used to love to dance."

"I still do. I—I'm just surprised you want to dance out here with so many people. With us being the center of attention."

Even though she was perfectly fine with the old Liam, this new Liam was quickly growing on her.

He pulled her close against his body. One of his hands rested on the center of her back and he took her hand in his as they swayed to *Your Secret Love*. Charlee laid her head against his chest, absorbing the light scent of his cologne as she got lost in the moment. It was as if the rest of the world faded away, and it was only the two of them rocking to the slow jam.

He was such a good dancer. Which wasn't a surprised. There wasn't much he wasn't good at. A perfectionist and a little OCD, he was meticulous about everything, which Charlee loved. He was everything she wasn't and they balanced each other perfectly.

When the song changed, they continued dancing until one song led into several others. This had been one of the best days she'd had in a long time. It probably had a lot to do with her finally taking a few days off from work and hanging out in one of the liveliest cities in the country. Yet, she knew it had everything to do with the man she was with.

Charlee lifted her head as they continued to rock to the music. "Now that we're committed to giving our relationship another try, what will that look like once we're back in Cincinnati?"

"Believe it or not, I actually haven't planned that far ahead."

"Whaaat? I can't believe it. You plot out everything. How is it that you haven't planned what happens next with us?"

"I didn't say I didn't plan what happens next," he said close to her ear, then sucked on her earlobe. His intentions were loud and clear.

A burst of desire shot through Charlee's body and her toes curled inside of her shoes. If that got her juices flowing, God help her when they got horizontal, which she was looking forward to.

"I'm a little out of my element here," Liam continued." All I know is that I love you, and I want us to try and make our relationship work this time."

Charlee studied him, wondering if he realized what he'd said. In the past, he'd always been good about expressing his feelings for her. There was no doubt in her mind that she was still in love with him, but to know their feelings were mutual meant everything.

She cupped his cheek and leaned in close. "I love you, too. I never stopped loving you."

Charlee kissed him with everything in her, hoping he could feel just how much she loved him.

When the kiss ended, Liam rested his forehead against hers for a minute before they stretched out on the blanket. Laying on their sides, they faced each other.

"Like you said earlier, we have things to work through. We just have to figure out where to start," he said, twirling a lock of her hair that had fallen out of her messy ponytail.

"I'll start by promising that I won't put my career before our relationship. Even if it means quitting my—"

"Whoa. No. You won't be quitting your job." When she started to speak, he held up his hand. "Charlee, I know how important your career is to you. I would never ask you to quit. That's not what came between us last time."

"It sorta was. Between the traveling, last-minute meetings, and I can keep going listing the things at work that hogged my time."

"People with just as demanding jobs figure out how to make relationships work. It's about commitment. We have to be committed enough to want to make this work."

"Yeah, you're right." Charlee often took on more responsibilities at work than she needed to. For now on, she'd make sure her priorities were in order.

"As long as we communicate better, and be straight with each other before situations get out of hand, we'll be okay."

"How about if we plan a date night once a week?" Charlee suggested. "That way we'll have a designated time that is all about us."

Liam nodded. "I'm good with that, and we have to spend time on the weekend together. I'm not saying it has to be a whole day, but we have to carve out time for us."

"I can commit to that."

"Now what about the traveling? How often are you out of town?"

"I don't have to travel. Well, not often. There might be times, like this trip, where I think I'd be the best person to close a deal. That's something I usually know in advance, though. We're talking maybe two or three times a year."

"And if you know about those trips ahead of time, I can travel with you."

Charlee couldn't help the smile that spread across her face. "I'd like that."

Liam pushed loose strands of hair behind her ear. "Let's head back to the hotel so that we can continue celebrating our reunion."

"I like that idea even more. I'm right behind you."

Chapter Eighteen

As they rode the elevator up to their hotel room, Liam could feel the anxiousness bouncing off of Charlee. He might want to get reacquainted with her body, but he didn't want to rush her into anything.

He moved the picnic basket to his other hand as they stepped off the elevator and then draped his arm around her shoulder.

"Listen. We don't have to do anything that you're not ready for."

She looked up at him, her brows furrowed. "What makes you think I'm not ready for whatever you're ready for?"

"I'm just saying that I don't want you to feel rushed into—"

"Oh, don't worry about me. You just better make sure you're ready, because the moment we get behind closed doors, I'm going to be all over you."

"Is that right?" He smiled down at her, not missing the merriment in her pretty brown eyes. "Well, I'm ready for you, baby."

Liam let her into the room and barely had a chance to set the basket down before Charlee shoved him up against a nearby wall. He sucked in a breath when her soft hands slid under his T-shirt and worked their way up his torso. Her touch sent waves of desire rallying through his body. If he didn't slow her roll, this would be over way before they got started good.

"I guess you weren't kidding about being ready," he said, tugging on the back of his collar and pulling the shirt over his head, tossing it to the floor. She wasn't the only one in a hurry to get them naked, but it had been a long time since they'd been together. He had no intention of rushing anything.

Charlee's hands stalled on his abs, and her gaze took in his upper body. She looked at him as if he was a piece of meat. "I didn't think your body could get any more perfect, but...man."

Liam chuckled at the awe in her voice. He removed the ponytail holder from her hair, tossing it on the nearby stand. He loved the way her curls tumbled around her shoulders. He slowly ran his fingers through her soft tresses, and gently gripped a handful, pulling her head back to give him full access to her neck.

She moaned as he trailed kisses from her jaw down to her bare shoulder and worked his way back up.

God, she smells good.

Liam's mouth covered hers hungrily as desire pumped through his veins. No other woman had the power to turn him on as fast as this woman...*his* woman. The woman he planned to spend the rest of his life with.

A groan slipped out, and a tremor shot through him when Charlee cupped his package. Kneading. Squeezing. Applying enough pressure to make him grip her hair tighter.

"Hey," he croaked, trying to stay in control.

"I've missed you," she murmured against his lips.

Liam ripped his mouth from hers and sucked in a breath. "If you keep that up..."

She went for his zipper, and he quickly grabbed her wrists. "Not yet. Not until I see all of you."

She gasped when he turned her suddenly, switching their position. With her back against the wall, he lifted her arms above her head and held them there with one hand.

"We're not rushing this." He spoke the words just above a whisper. Now all he had to do was get his body to cooperate. He was hard enough to punch a hole through his zipper, but he was determined to take his time with her. No doubt she could feel his erection pressed against her lower stomach, which was fine with him. He wanted her to feel what she did to him.

"Liam..."

Not giving her a chance to say another word, he kissed her with a need that was as fierce as a multiple-vortex tornado. His free hand roamed slowly down her body, gliding over her curves as his tongue tangled with hers.

Charlee moaned into his mouth, squirming against him.

He said they weren't going to rush this, but as bad as he wanted her, he honestly couldn't guarantee that he'd be able to go slow. Liam had fantasized about having her again more times than he could count. If anyone would've told him that they'd get back together, he wouldn't have believed them. Normally, when he was done with something or someone, he was done. But there had always been something special about Charlee that he couldn't explain.

Now, after spending the last twenty-four hours with her, he knew without a doubt what that something was.

She was *the one*. It was plain and simple, and he wanted to kick himself for denying the inevitable for so long.

"Liam, I want you now," Charlee said in a rush as soon as he moved his mouth from hers.

Still holding her arms above her head, he reached behind her neck and undid the tie of her dress with one hand. The top of the garment fell down, revealing full breasts that were practically spilling over the top of her black strapless bra.

He swallowed hard, trying to throttle the powerful current raging through his body at the sight of her.

"I want you, too," he finally said, his hammering heart beating so loud against his chest, people in the next room could probably hear it.

With a flick of his wrist, he undid the bra and tossed it to the floor. Then he stood there, gawking. Taking in all of her beauty. She was even more drool-worthy than he remembered.

"You're…you're breathtaking."

"And you're taking too long."

He laughed and released her arms. Before she could move, Liam looped his arm around her waist, bringing her close and cupped one of her breasts. She was more than a handful, and he savored the feel of her in his palm. His body tightened with need as he brushed the pad of his thumb over her nipple before lowering his head. Sucking and teasing, he swirled his tongue around the hardened peak until she withered against him.

Charlee whimpered, her hands cradling his head. "Liam, I…can't take…too much." She wiggled against him. "It's been too long…" Her words trailed off when he moved to her other breast, his teeth grazing her nipple.

He ignored her plea, wanting to savor all of her.

"Okay…okay," she panted, still squirming against him, only making him that much more hungry for her. "Please, baby, we—"

"You're so damn irresistible."

Liam got his fill before he finally lifted his head. Staring down into her lust-filled eyes, a sensuous charge passed between them. Something so mind-blowingly powerful that it shook him to the depths of his soul. He didn't even want to try and put meaning behind the intenseness of the moment. All he wanted to do was love on this gorgeous woman and take them both to a place of no return.

He stripped the dress from her lithe body, leaving her in only a tiny pair of black panties.

A low growl started in his chest and worked its way up his throat. Charlee squeaked when he suddenly lifted her, holding tightly around his neck as he carried her across the room. Liam didn't stop until he reached the bed.

"Don't move," he said when he laid her down. He quickly dug his wallet from the back pocket of his jeans and pulled out a condom. Dropping the wallet, he didn't care where it landed. His mind was solely on getting out of the rest of his clothes.

He watched as Charlee lifted her hips off the bed and started sliding her panties down her shapely legs. He almost swallowed his tongue at the sight she made sprawled out on the bed.

Going slow is out of the question.

She looked at Liam through lowered lids as he quickly sheathed himself. The man's body was total perfection from his muscular chest to his ripped abs, on down to his long, thick erection. Slowly and seductively, he climbed onto the bed, his eyes taking in every inch of her body.

She tried not to squirm under his perusal, but her skin tingled at the attention. Love sparkled in his intense, dark eyes, reflecting everything she felt inside. Love, lust, need. She and Liam never had a problem in the bedroom, and she couldn't wait to see if their hot kisses would extend to even hotter lovemaking.

Without a word, he moved between her thighs, spreading them wider with his legs as he hovered above her. When he lowered his head and covered her mouth with his, she wrapped her arms around his neck. A ripple of excitement charged through her as he eased into her heat, inch by delicious inch.

He felt incredible. She feared she'd come before they even got started good. She hadn't been kidding when she told him that it had been a long time. Her body was starving for the connection. A connection that only he could provide.

As Liam moved inside of her, he nipped then licked an area just below her ear before sucking the same spot, probably marking his territory. All the while, he rotated his hips, first moving slowly as he slid in and out of her, then picking up speed, going deeper and harder with each thrust.

Being with this man again, like this, was more than she could've ever hoped for. Fate had brought them together, and Charlee had no intentions of ever letting him go again. This man was divinely made for her and the person she was meant to be with. No one else would ever do.

Their moans blended in the quietness of the room as they got lost in the euphoria of their lovemaking. Every touch, moan, groan, and thrust brought them even closer together. Their bodies moved in perfect harmony as Charlee lifted her hips off the bed, matching him stroke for stroke.

"Ahh, baby," Liam ground out and holding her right hip higher, his fingers burning into her thigh. He plowed into her harder as his other hand clutched the headboard.

"Oh, yes," Charlee breathed, her hands gripping his firm butt as she struggled to hold on. "Liam," she started, but with another thrust, a powerful current shot through every cell in her body. She bucked against him, shaking violently as a downpour of fiery sensations sent her completely over the edge.

Seconds later, Liam stiffened. His release was right behind hers and the guttural rumble of his groan pierced the air before he collapsed on top of her.

Mercy.

Yep, they were as good together as she remembered, Charlee thought as she wrapped her arms around him and held tight. Their ragged breaths blended. Neither moved. They laid in that position for what seemed like an hour, but was probably mere minutes, basking in the afterglow of their lovemaking.

Again, Charlee was experiencing a dream-like moment with him, and a deep feeling of peace fell over her. She wanted to say something, anything that could describe the intensity of how full her heart was. Words didn't come. She was too emotionally and sexually filled to speak as minutes ticked by.

"You're amazing," Liam said, nuzzling her neck before rolling onto his back, pulling her to his side.

Charlee snuggled into him, flinging a limp arm across his midsection, too tired to do much else. "Ditto, babe."

She was so in love with this man, and the more time they spent together, the more time she wanted with him. If only they didn't have to return to their everyday lives. If only they could stay on vacation forever.

That was her last thought before drifting off to sleep.

Chapter Nineteen

Liam couldn't remember the last time he'd slept so well. He'd been awake for at least an hour while Charlee lay with her head on his chest and one of her smooth legs draped over his. The soft curves of her body nestled against him felt so good that he wanted her all over again.

Their night of lovemaking had exceeded anything he had ever experienced, even with her. It was as if they hadn't been a part for almost two years, picking up where they left off. Neither able to get enough of the other. Sex between them had always been powerfully intense, physically, and emotionally. But last night...

He released a contented sigh.

So much for taking their reunion slow. How crazy was he to think he could take anything slow with this force of nature? From the moment they'd met, Liam felt more alive with this woman than he ever had in his life. Taking risks with no regard for consequences was how he operated whenever she was around.

She was his other half. His rib. His heart. The woman who completed him. It was a wonder he had survived the last two years without her.

"Go back to sleep," Charlee said, her sleep-filled, husky voice catching him by surprise. "I can hear your mind working."

Liam smiled and shook his head. He pulled her on top of him, but groaned when she rubbed up against his morning wood.

"Mmm, yeah. Good morning," she crooned, kissing him while continuing to move seductively.

"You keep wiggling like that, I'm going to slide right in," he said against her mouth, cupping her butt cheeks and squeezing. Lucky for them he had thought to pick up some condoms on the way back to the hotel after their boat ride.

"I would love to get something started, but I think I'm going to need a long soak in the tub before we do more bumping and grinding."

Liam's hands stilled on her rear. "You're soar?" That was a dumb question. By their third round, in the middle of the night, even he had been wiped out.

"More than I care to admit."

She gasped when Liam rolled them onto their sides. Chest to chest and thigh to thigh, he held her close not wanting her to move away.

"Why didn't you tell me you were sore?"

"It's not that big of a deal. No way was I going to let a little soreness stop me from loving on you. Which is why we both should still be asleep. Getting refueled for another round, later."

"Much, much later. I need you at one hundred percent. Are you hungry?"

She shook her head, curls falling into her face with the move. "Too tired. Besides, it's too early to eat."

"Early? It's almost nine o'clock. We need to get up and going if you want to squeeze in everything you've planned for us."

He rarely slept past six, able to operate on as little as five hours of sleep. Usually, he would've been up, worked out and had two cups of coffee by now.

"But first, I'll get that bath water started." Liam made a move to get up, but Charlee stopped him.

"Not yet, I just want us to stay like this for a little while longer. She cupped his jaw with her hand, running her fingers over his full beard.

Liam covered her hand, then turned it and placed a kiss in her palm. "I missed this."

He missed everything about her. The way she stared into his eyes, love brimming in their depths. He missed holding and caressing her, having her hugged up against him.

How had he let her go? The woman stirred something so incredibly intense within him. There was no way he was letting her go again.

"I want you to meet my family." The words were out of Liam's mouth before he could stop them, but he meant it. He was ready to introduce her to his world.

After a slight hesitation, Charlee said, "Okay, but why now? Before you said that you didn't want them in your business. What's changed?"

"It's time." He gently ran his hand up and down the side of her body as he stared into her eyes. "I should've done it before when we were together. It's just that…"

Now that he was thinking about it, his reasons back then seemed a little lame.

"You said that you didn't want your family in your business, but I sensed there was more to it."

Liam sighed. He rolled onto his back and propped one of his arms beneath his head. He wrapped the other around Charlee.

"That was part of it," he said. "You have to understand. My family is…a lot. Unless you've ever been a part of a large, close-knit family, you don't understand how easy it is for people to get into your business. Don't get me wrong, sometimes it's good. Knowing you have uncles, aunts, and cousins, who have your back is a wonderful thing. Other times, it's just a…pain."

Charlee nodded, her disheveled hair brushing against his skin and tickling his chest. "I can understand that, especially with an introvert like you. It probably can get a little overwhelming when everyone is together. But what's the other reason you kept me away from them?"

In most cases, the family didn't bring people they were dating around until it was a sure thing. Until that person knew that relationship was heading toward marriage.

Liam wondered if there was a part of him back then that knew that he and Charlee wouldn't make it. Then again, once they were engaged, he had planned on introducing her. It just hadn't worked out. But now, he had no intention of ever letting her go again.

Charlee made small, circular motions on his stomach with her finger, pulling him back to the present. Liam really didn't want to tell her about what happened with his cousin, mainly because it was in the past like Martina had said. Yet, there was still a part of him deep down inside that harbored the betrayal. He gave her the cliff notes version of that particular Sunday brunch when he caught his college sweetheart with his cousin.

"Oh, my goodness. That had to be *awful*. Even if it happened years ago, that type of disloyalty is hard to get past. I'm sure the woman is no longer around, but do you ever talk to your cousin?"

"No. I saw him one Sunday a few months ago, but we don't keep in touch. He and his brothers live in Chicago."

"So, you didn't take me around any of them thinking that the same thing would happen? That I would betray you like that?"

Liam glanced down and met her gaze. "I think a small part of me was afraid it could happen again. Never in a million years would I expect someone in my *family* to treat me the way he had. As for you, I trust you explicitly."

"I'm glad, because I would *never* step out on you. As for your family getting all up in your...our business, that won't happen unless we allow it."

"Yeah, that's what you think. You don't know my cousin, Martina. The woman is like a bloodhound when she's digging for info on us. She hunts down good gossip for shits and giggles."

Charlee fell out laughing. "She's not that bad. I met MJ once when Rayne had me drop Stormy off at Martina's house to play with her daughter. She seemed nice."

"Until you get to know her," Liam cracked, but in all honesty, he had mad love for his cousin.

"I like your family, at least those I've met through Rayne. She absolutely adores the Jenkins' clan."

"And they're crazy about her just like I know they're going to love you."

"I'm looking forward to meeting them, but right now, I'm hungry. Maybe you're right. We should probably get this day started."

"Okay, but first…"

Liam flipped Charlee onto her back, then trailed feathery kisses down the center of her amazing body. She squirmed beneath him as he continued traveling south toward the apex of her thighs.

"Let me see if I can do a little somethin' somethin' to help ease some of your soreness."

Chapter Twenty

Hours later, Liam and Charlee stepped into the coffee shop that they'd visited at least five times within the last forty-eight hours. Charlee couldn't walk into a coffee shop now without recalling the scene between him and Everett. A turning point in her and Liam's relationship that she would forever be grateful for.

Liam held her close, his arm around her body with his hand resting on her hip. Their morning had been just as eventful as the night before, and it had been hard to leave the hotel. Had it been up to her, they'd still be lounging in bed, feasting on each other.

"Should we eat a little something here and then plan for a big lunch later?" Liam asked, pulling Charlee out of her thoughts as they inched forward in the line.

Throughout the night and right before her bubble bath, they had snacked on the leftovers from their picnic. "I think that's a good idea. I'm not all that hungry, but I can go for a small latte and a croissant."

"Good morning. What can I get you two today?" the cashier asked.

As Liam placed their order, Charlee glanced around the cozy shop. Her attention landed on an older couple who she'd seen in there a few times. Apparently, one of them had a love for coffee just as much as Liam had.

The woman smiled and gave a slight wave, and Charlee nodded a greeting back. She wondered if when she and Liam got that age if they'd be hanging out in coffee shops all day.

"I'll go and find us a table," she said when they stepped off to the side to wait for their order.

The place wasn't that big, and all the tables were taken. No one seemed in a hurry to leave anytime soon. Even though Liam probably would kill her for what she was about to do, she approached the older couple she had spotted a moment ago. They were seated at a small table that had four chairs.

"Hi," she said. "I know this is probably an odd request, but can we join you two?"

"Of course, dear," the woman said, moving to the chair closer to the man instead of where she was sitting across from him. "We'd love the company. I've seen you and your young man here a few times."

"Yes, he likes the coffee here." Charlee sat in the chair next to the woman, just as Liam approached the table. "Hey, babe. These nice people agreed to share their table with us since there's nothing else available."

"Yeah, come and join us. Make yourself comfortable," the older man piped up for the first time since Charlee had approached them. He stood and extended his hand, and Liam shook it. "I'm Mark and this is my wife Josie."

"Nice to meet you both. I'm Liam and I assume you've already met Charlee."

"Not officially, but we've seen each other in here a few times."

"Liam, I guess you and I have something in common." Mark lifted his cup. "We both enjoy a good cup of coffee. This place has the best in the city."

"I'm finding that out." Liam draped his arm on the back of Charlee's chair, his hand grazing her back. She loved having his hands anywhere on her, and all morning he had found every excuse to touch her.

Her cheeks heated, and she lowered her gaze, staring down at her fingers interlocked in her lap, as she recalled all the ways he had touched her. If she hadn't already been hooked on him, she would've been now after their lovemaking marathon. The man was...perfection. Their reconciliation had to work this time because she didn't know what she would do if he walked out of her life again. There was no way she could go back to things as they were.

"Since we're both retired, we usually ride into the city a few times a week to hang out. Even more this week since the weather has been so nice," Josie said, cutting into Charlee's thoughts.

For the next few minutes, conversation flowed easily as if they'd all known each other for years. Liam and Mark discussed their jobs, realizing they had much in common. Mark had been a graphic designer for forty years and occasionally did work on the side, while Josie had recently retired from family law.

"You two are a lovely couple. How long have you been together?" Josie asked.

Charlee glanced at Liam, unsure how to answer and found him studying her. His New York Yankee's baseball cap was pulled down low, but not low enough that she couldn't see love radiating in his eyes.

"We've been together off and on for a couple of years," he said, holding her hand under the table.

Her heart melted a little more. There had been moments since running into him at the bar, where it felt as if no time had passed between them. His words that day in his kitchen, about them not being able to go back, came to mind. They might not be able to go back, but it definitely felt as if they had picked up where they left off.

"Mark and I have been married almost forty years." Josie smiled at her husband whose love for her reflected on his face.

"We used to see each other on the subway every morning, until one day I decided to invite her out for coffee," Mark explained. "Six weeks later we were married."

"Wow, you guys didn't waste any time," Liam said.

Josie shrugged. "What can I say? I'm easy."

They all laughed, and Mark kissed her cheek.

"When you know…you just know."

"And I knew." Josie stared lovingly at her husband before turning her gaze to Liam. "Just like I think you know. Maybe you should marry your lovely woman."

Whoa. Charlee hadn't expected that and didn't dare look at Liam, hating he was being put on the spot.

"Maybe I should," he said without missing a beat.

Charlee's head jerked toward him, shocked by his words. She expected him to laugh or do something that would let her know that he was joking. That didn't happen. His expression was as serious as usual.

In her heart, she knew she would never love another man. But, from the moment Liam told her that he wanted her back, Charlee remained cautiously optimistic. She didn't want to get overly excited that she might finally get her happily-ever-after with him. Even when he mentioned her meeting his family, she agreed but didn't want to get her hopes up that that would somehow lead to marriage.

"While you're in town, if you decide you want to make your union official, give me a call." Josie handed Liam a business card and he chuckled, turning the card for Charlee to read.

I'll marry you, was in bold, script lettering across the top. Her name and registered marriage officiant beneath it.

"Don't let her pressure you into doing something you might not be ready for," Mark said. "She's always trying to marry people off."

Josie nudged shoulders with her husband. "Oh, hush. Anyone can tell that they're in love. Why not get married?"

It wasn't often that Charlee was left speechless. This was one of those moments. She'd marry Liam in a heartbeat but didn't want him pressured into asking her again.

Josie proceeded to tell them how many couples she had married over the years, with Mark piping in with details. By the time the conversation was over, the two had enlightened them on where they could pick up a marriage license, the cost, and how to get married.

"So, if you need my services to marry your woman, just call."

"I'll keep that in mind," Liam said non-committal, glancing at the card again before slipping it into the back pocket of his jeans.

"Thanks for the information," Charlee finally said, a little amused by the whole exchange. To be honest, she was a bit intrigued by the idea of eloping. "We should probably get going. Thank you so much for letting us share your table."

"It was a pleasure to meet you both," Mark said as they all stood.

Josie touched Charlee's arm. "Maybe we'll see the two of you before you leave town."

"You never know." Liam gave Charlee's hand a little tug and guided her out the door. They were planning to do an uptown bus tour to check out a few museums and the Empire State Building Observatory. She'd been to New York a few times, but that was the one place she had never toured.

"Well, that was…interesting," she said once they were outside.

Liam slipped on his sunglasses. "Yeah, it was. We go in for coffee and end up learning anything we wanted to know about eloping in New York. But hey, anything can happen."

"Ha! Yeah, right. Like you'd ever consider eloping."

"Hey, it could happen. I agreed to go along with anything while we're on this trip, remember?"

"Oh, yeah. I remember."

They headed up the street to hop on the double-decker bus, and Charlee played Liam's words around in her mind.

Even though he'd been going with the flow while they were in New York, he would never consider eloping. Besides, they had just reunited. There was no way they could get married.

But it was a fun thought.

*

Charlee sat on the foot of the bed, toed off her high-heeled sandals and then flopped back. Her arms spread wide on top of the comforter as she stared at the ceiling.

It was almost midnight, and they had just returned to the hotel. Between touring the city for much of the day and then attending a Broadway show, her energy was wiped. Yet, she couldn't shut off her brain. Thoughts ran rampant through her mind, bouncing from one idea or thought to another.

Liam. Her thoughts for the last two days had mostly centered around him. Mainly because these had been some of the best days that she'd had in years. Could they really return home and continue seeing each other? Or would their day-to-day lives get in the way? Actually, it wasn't his life that she was concerned about. It was hers.

She vowed that she could put their relationship first and not let her work consume every waking day, but could she really? Liam told her the other night that she could have it all. Him, her career, and a family. However, Charlee worried that she'd goof it up and lose him for good.

"I want this to work more than anything," she mumbled to herself. "I can, no, I will put our relationship first."

Charlee sat up. Her gaze darted to the bathroom door as it opened, and Liam stepped out. His hand was on his tie-knot, moving it side to side until it loosened and he pulled it over his head. Laying it on the dresser, he started undoing the buttons on his light-blue dress shirt.

He was such a handsome man. She could look at him all day. It didn't matter what he was doing, he snagged her attention without even trying.

"You haven't said much since we left the show," he said, studying her. "What's wrong? You okay?"

She stood and walked to him. "I was thinking."

"Oh, boy." He shook his head and removed his shirt, leaving him in a white T-shirt. "Every time you start with, *I was thinking*, I get nervous."

Charlee laughed and punched him in the arm. "Be quiet. I'm serious."

"Okay. Okay, I'm listening. What's going on in that beautiful head of yours?"

"I love you."

He didn't respond. Only stood there looking at her as if waiting for her to say something else.

She wanted that to sink in before she continued. Before she could say anything else, Liam wrapped his arms around her waist and pulled her against his body. Then his lips touched hers in a slow, soul-stirring kiss.

"I love you too, sweetheart." He rested his forehead against hers. "What I feel for you..." He stopped speaking and shook his head as if strangled by emotion.

Charlee understood. The love she had for this man was a bit overwhelming. In a good way.

"What I feel for you," Liam cupped her face, "is like nothing I've ever experienced with anyone. It's like I can breathe better when you're with me. Like...everything is brighter with you around. I know I keep saying it, but baby... I. Have. Missed. You."

"Aw, Liam." Charlee bit her bottom lip, fighting to hold back a sob. "That's the sweetest thing you've ever said to me. You have no idea how much that means to me, and I feel the same about you."

One of his rare smiles appeared, and his whole face lit up. "I think I know. We have a chance to get it right this time."

"That's what I was thinking. Actually, I was thinking about something else, too." She eased out of his hold and sucked in a long breath before releasing it slowly to get her nerves under control.

Liam shoved his hands into the front pockets of his suit pants. The smile covering his mouth only moments ago— gone.

She needed to just say what was on her mind before he assumed what she had to say was something bad. It wasn't. Maybe a little crazy, but not bad.

"Will you marry me?" she blurted, glad the words found their way to the surface.

Liam's brows shot up, and he opened his mouth to speak. Then closed it looking a little shell-shocked.

"Since I love you, and you love me, why not get married? We want the same things. We want to be together for a lifetime. We want a family. We're in love. We're both committed to making our relationship work."

The words flew from her mouth so fast, Charlee wasn't sure if she was making sense.

"And we have a person who will marry us at a moment's notice. I love you more than anything, and I want you to be my husband. I want you to spend the rest of your life with me. Marry me."

After a long hesitation, he said, "When do you want to get married?"

She gave a slight shrug. "I'm free tomorrow. How about you?"

Liam chuckled. "You know this is crazy, right?"

"I know, but life is short. There are no guarantees. Besides, you agreed to go along with whatever I wanted to do while we're here. I say we elope."

"And I say…I can't wait to marry you."

His words hit her like a two-by-four against the head. Charlee screamed. Leaped into his arms and kissed him hard. Even though she had asked, she didn't actually think he'd say yes.

"But, there's only one problem with your plan," Liam said when he set her on her feet. "I don't have a ring for you."

"Um, about that."

She hurried back to the bed where she had left her purse and dumped the contents in order to get to the inside zipper. She pulled out the small, velvet pouch that she'd been carrying around with her for almost two years.

"Will this work?"

Liam stared at the three-carat princess cut diamond ring then looked at her, and then back at the ring. "You kept it?"

"Of course, I kept it. Did you think I would pawn it or something? When you didn't take it back, I had planned to be buried with it."

That night Liam broke up with her, Charlee thought she would never recover. The first few weeks he wouldn't even accept her calls. He wouldn't let her apologize for ruining their relationship. Eventually, he answered one of her calls, and she asked that they meet so that she could give back the ring. He didn't want it.

Now here they were, back together and possibly getting married.

Fate.

No matter how she looked at it, Charlee knew their chance meeting in New York, was fate taking over.

"So, will you marry me?" she asked again.

He took the ring from her fingers and studied it before meeting her gaze. "Yeah, I'll marry you. Anytime. Anywhere."

Chapter Twenty-One

"Married?" Jerry and Rayne yelled in unison, their eyes wide and mouths hanging open.

"How?"

"When?"

They both talked at once, shooting out one question after another while Charlee and Liam stood on their front stoop.

"Can we at least come in?" Liam asked, giving Charlee an *I told you so* look.

He had been adamant about telling his family and her father at the same time during the next Jenkins' family brunch, which was that coming Sunday.

Charlee wasn't like him. When she was excited about something, she wanted to shout it out to the universe. Liam, on the other hand, could take a secret to his grave and think nothing of it.

That morning, Josie married them in Central Park. The area where they had their picnic had been the perfect spot with the fountain and the lake as their backdrop. Just thinking about how remarkable the fifteen-minute ceremony was made Charlee's heart sing.

We're married. The words kept playing around in her head for the last eight hours. They had picked up the marriage license the morning after she had proposed, but had to wait twenty-four hours before they could get married. Which meant they were married only hours before their plane took off for Cincinnati.

"We should let your asses stay out there," Jerry said, and Rayne elbowed him.

They expected everyone to be surprised, especially since they hadn't been dating. Yet, Charlee thought they would get a different reception from their best friends.

"Come in," Rayne said, moving away from the door. "The kids are asleep. We can talk in the family room."

Charlee and Liam followed her into the large room. There was comfortable furniture and a big screen television, as well as a few toys in a nearby corner of the space.

They sat on the sofa next to Rayne while Jerry sat in his recliner.

"Okay, tell us everything," Rayne said.

"Not *everything*," Jerry added with a frown. "I just want to know why you had to just up and get married when you weren't even dating."

"There's not much to tell. We hooked up in New York, toured the city, ate a lot and got married," Liam said, scowling at Jerry as if he wanted to punch him.

Charlee wasn't sure what silent conversation they were having, but something was transpiring between them.

"What else you want to know?" Liam growled.

Charlee's heart sunk. They were supposed to be celebrating, not defending themselves. "Why are you mad?" she asked Jerry.

He had always treated her like a sister and was the main one telling her that Liam was still in love with her. She wasn't sure where this animosity she was feeling was coming from.

"I'm not mad!" he said, then huffed out a breath. "I'm shocked. One minute, you guys are glaring at each other, the next—"

"I've never glared at Liam," Charlee interrupted, then looked at her husband. He covered her hand with his and gave it a reassuring squeeze.

"Yeah, but too bad the blockhead sitting next to you can't say the same thing." Jerry leaned forward, his elbows on his thighs as he looked from her to Liam. "There is no doubt in my mind that you two love each other, but marriage is serious. You can't just...just up and do something like that without knowing what you're getting into. There's a lot to take into consideration."

"Says the person who vowed never to get married," Liam said, an angry bite in his tone. "Man, we are grown ass people. We don't give a sh—"

"Okay, you know what? Let's tone it down a notch," Rayne said. "Better yet, Jerry, why don't you and Liam take your issues downstairs, and Charlee and I can talk up here."

The moment they were gone, Charlee shot out of her seat and paced the length of the room. "I at least thought you would be happy for us. You know how much I love him."

"I know. I also know that you do things on a whim all the time and don't consider consequences until after the fact. I'm afraid that come tomorrow, you guys might have a change of heart."

"Rayne, we are crazy about each other. This is not just a whim. This is about love."

"Love is one thing, but marriage is a whole different beast. It's not something to take lightly."

"I thought you loved being married."

"I adore being married, and I would walk through fire for my husband. He's my everything, and more than I could have ever wished for."

"Then what's the problem? That's exactly how I feel about Liam. I've loved him for over two years, from the first date we went on. I knew then that he was special and that I had struck gold in meeting him. And I know he loves me. Running into each other in New York was like fate giving us that push we needed to see this relationship through."

"I'm like Jerry. I know how much you two love each other, but you guys had some real issues in your relationship before. There's no way that could've been resolved in only a few days."

Charlee huffed out a breath and dropped down on the sofa, folding her arms across her chest. She knew marriage wasn't easy. Nothing in life was easy. Yet, she was confident that they'd made the right decision. They were adults, knew each other better than anyone, and were both determined to make their marriage work, and that's what she explained to Rayne.

This was supposed to be one of the happiest days of her life. She finally married the man who held her heart. Never would she have thought that she'd have to defend her decision to her best friend.

Suddenly, Charlee wanted to run downstairs, grab Liam and head back to New York where they could do whatever the heck they wanted and not have to answer or defend themselves to anyone.

"Did you marry Liam to get the CEO position?"

Charlee gasped. "Of course not!" she bit out, surprised and disappointed at her friend's accusatory tone.

Sure, she had joked about finding a husband in order to get the job, but never intended on doing anything like that.

"For your information, the CEO position hasn't crossed my mind since running into him in New York."

"And that brings me to another point. You have worked so hard to get where you are in the company. Your career is everything to you, and those are your words, not mine. If you struggled to juggle your relationship and your job before when you guys were together, what makes you think it's going to be any easier now? You'll have more responsibilities if your father slides you into that position."

"I'm not worried about that. I'm already planning to do more delegating. If that doesn't work, I'll quit before I let work come between Liam and me again! Can't you just be happy for me?" Charlee sobbed, unsure why she was getting emotional. Rarely did she care what others thought, but this wasn't just anyone. This was Rayne, her best friend who was more like a sister.

Charlee swiped at a rogue tear that slid down her cheek.

"Aw, honey. Don't cry. Of course, I'm happy for you, and I can't wait to hear the details." Rayne pulled her in for a hug. "I only want the best for you and Liam, and I don't want either of you to get hurt again."

"We won't."

"Yeah, you say that now." Rayne slowly released her and got up to grab a few tissues from a nearby Kleenex box and handed them to Charlee. "But what if—"

"We won't get hurt. We love each other too much for that to happen. We're going to make it this time and have an amazing life together. You'll see."

*

"I can't wrap my brain around the two of you getting married after only hanging out a few days. It doesn't make sense," Jerry said, as he leaned over the pool table. He knocked the five ball into the side pocket and the seven into the right corner pocket. He had always been the best at pool out of all of their cousins.

"It doesn't have to make sense to you." Liam set up to take his shot after Jerry missed. "What Charlee and I do is no one's damn business."

"You know she's like a sister to me, and I think she's good for you. Getting married all of a sudden isn't like you. The man who plans everything meticulously. Nah, I'm not buying that you married her on a whim. Were you drunk?"

"No."

"Were you guys secretly dating before you went to New York?

"No."

"Is she pregnant?"

Liam glared at him. "No!"

"Then what happened? Why the rush? Why not date a few months? Hell, even a few weeks would've been better than a couple of days."

Liam missed his next shot after making two.

His cousin was right. He wasn't the type to go off course, drive outside of the lines, or do something like getting married on impulse. There were moments he still couldn't believe he went through with Charlee's idea. Normally, he was the logical one. The one who reeled her back in when she got ahead of herself. Not this time. This time the idea seemed…perfect. From the moment they said, *I do*, he didn't have any regrets. No second thoughts. No desire to get their marriage annulled. Hell, he would marry her all over again if he had to.

"You know what? If it were left up to me, I would have told you and Rayne about our marriage along with the rest of the family on Sunday," he finally said, irritated by the conversation.

Jerry chuckled, and then missed his next shot. "In the words of Martina, I can't wait for Sunday brunch. The shit is definitely going to fly. You gon' drop some mess like that on your parents…in front of everyone? Oh man, and don't get me started on Kingslee. He's probably going to pull out his shotgun."

That was probably the only thing Liam regretted. He wasn't a traditional guy. He hadn't asked Charlee's father for her hand in marriage the first time and wouldn't have done it this time had they not eloped. However, with Charlee being an only child and only daughter, Kingslee would've wanted to walk her down the aisle.

Maybe they'd have a small ceremony in the near future if Charlee wanted.

Jerry leaned on the edge of the pool table. "You're going to have a lot of explaining to do."

"Like I said. What we do is nobody's business." Liam took his shot and made it. He set up for the next one but stopped and straightened. "Oh, and the next time you upset my *wife* the way you did upstairs, I'm going to beat your ass."

Jerry stared at him for a moment, then burst out laughing, bumping the pool table and knocking the balls all around. Once he finally sobered, he wiped at his eyes with the heel of his hand.

"Man, you're a trip. A few weeks ago, you'd pitch a fit if I said her name in your presence. Now, you're referring to her as your *wife.*"

"I'm serious, Jay. You can talk crazy to me, but I don't want you upsetting her, especially not about this. She's happy, and I plan to keep her that way."

Jerry nodded. "Okay, messed that up. You guys just caught me off guard, but I gotta ask. Why'd you decide to get married on the fly like that?"

Visions of Charlee flashed through Liam's mind. Her laugh. Her hypnotic eyes. That smile that made him want to smile. Her vibrant personality that could light up a room without her speaking a word. All that played around in his head. Yet, it was the way she made him feel that had him prepared to do anything for her.

"Because she's *the one,*" he finally said. "I knew it two years ago when I asked her to marry me, and I know it now. She's the one for me, and this time I went for it."

Silence filled the room. Liam knew Jerry understood exactly how he felt. He'd gone through similar emotions and unexplained actions once he realized Rayne was the one for him. Now Liam knew without a doubt that the so-called Jenkins' men myth wasn't a myth at all. When they found the woman for them, they just knew, and to hell with common sense.

After a slight hesitation, Jerry said, "I get it." He chuckled while rubbing the back of his neck. "Yeah, I *totally* get it, and I'm happy for you, man. I'm glad you and Charlee found your way back to each other." They hugged, and Jerry pounded him on the back. "But I still can't wait until Sunday. Brunch is going to be *lit.*"

175

"Whatever, man. Just make sure you keep your trap shut until then."

Chapter Twenty-Two

"Your *wife?*"

"You did what?"

"Oh, snap!"

"Get out of here!"

The noise volume in Liam's grandparents' enormous kitchen was almost deafening, causing family members who were spread out over other parts of the house to rush into the room.

Questions and comments flew at him and Charlee from all directions. Before they could answer one, another was thrown their way. It was safe to assume that Jerry and Rayne hadn't said anything to anyone. Liam wasn't sure if that was a good thing or if he should've allowed them to start spreading the news. At least then, he could've fielded phone calls and not have to deal with everyone at once.

The past week had been busy with them moving Charlee into his place. At the airport, after they were married, they started working on logistics of how to join their lives and homes. She agreed to move in with him since his place was bigger, and they planned to rent out her condo, furnishings and all.

177

There was still a lot for them to figure out, but so far, married life was terrific. Now all they had to do was get through the next couple of hours with his family. At least they had time before her father showed up. He'd had to make a quick trip out of town and was flying in from Florida. He wouldn't get back to Cincinnati for at least another couple of hours.

Charlee handed Liam the cake that she insisted on picking up on the way to the brunch. He set it on the oversized kitchen island that they were standing next to. She was in for a gentle tongue lashing when his grandmother found out it wasn't homemade.

"This is quite a surprise. Why didn't you tell us you were seeing each other?" Liam's mom, Kirsten, asked after hugging Charlee and then him. "Then again, I should've known. I remember catching Liam staring at you more than once at Jerry and Rayne's baby shower."

Charlee glanced Liam's way. When she smiled at him, his heart kicked against his chest. Everything between them unfolded so fast. Yet, he was sure they'd done the right thing. It had been a long time since he'd been as happy as he was now, and he wanted to maintain the feeling for the rest of their lives.

"Yeah, that day your mom suspected something was up. She wanted me to pump you for information," Liam's father Lee Jenkins said, pulling Liam into a hug. "Congratulations, son. Can't wait to hear the details." The words were spoken only loud enough for Liam to hear before his father embraced Charlee.

He and his dad had always had a good relationship. They could often be found on the golf course or somewhere fishing. Since neither of them were big talkers, they enjoyed each other's company while being content with quiet moments.

Liam was reminded of a lively conversation during a round of golf. His father had once told him that he had fallen in love with Liam's mother the first time he asked her out for dinner. She turned him down. He kept asking, getting more creative with his methods and she finally said yes. Less than a year later, they were married.

As their parents went back to fixing their plates, Jada approached Liam and Charlee. She was smiling like she had just learned the secret of how to be cute and comfortable in high heels. She stopped in front of Charlee.

"All I have to say is, I am so glad he married someone who enjoys shopping as much as I do!" She hugged Charlee, and they both burst into giggles. She then turned to Liam. "You've been holding out, big brother."

Liam smiled and accepted a hug from her, remembering Jada's speech in Peyton's living room.

Give her a chance. Don't expect her to be perfect.

It was the first time his sister had ever given him advice, and he was glad she had. That conversation and the thousands of thoughts that kept invading his mind about Charlee was just the push he needed to follow his heart. No longer did he have to fantasize about what it would be like to have her as his wife. She was now his reality.

"I *knew* there was someone special." Jada poked him in the chest. "I just didn't know it was Charlee. You did good, big brother."

"I guess I need to add another line-item to our family budget if you two are planning to shop together," he grumbled good-naturedly.

Jada noticed the cake. "Why'd you guys bring dessert?"

"Charlee insisted."

"I couldn't come empty handed. We stopped on the way here to pick it up."

Jada grinned. "Girrl, I suggest you hide it before—"

"All right, move along and let me meet my newest granddaughter," Katherine Jenkins, the matriarch of the family, said.

Jada's grin turned into full-blown laughter and Liam groaned again.

179

"Well, too late, sister-in-law. You're going to have to find out the hard way."

They both knew how funny-acting their grandmother was about store-bought baked goods. Not that anything was wrong with them. She just insisted that homemade tasted better.

"So, this is your wife," Liam's grandmother said, a twinkle in her eye as she reached for Charlee. "Welcome to the family, sweetie."

She hugged Charlee than patted Liam on the cheek. Her warm smile was the one thing he missed about not attending brunch on a regular basis. His grandmother was in her eighties but still got around better than some people who were twenty or thirty years younger.

"Thank you, Mrs. Jenkins. It's a pleasure to meet you," Charlee said and picked up the dessert. "I hope you don't mind, but I didn't want to come to brunch empty-handed."

Katherine frowned, then looked at Liam. "You didn't tell her that I don't allow store-bought cakes in this house?"

Charlee's brows shot up, and her eyes rounded as wide as saucers. Liam tried not to laugh at her horrified expression, but couldn't stop his lips from twitching.

"Come on, Gram." He put his other arm around her and kissed her cheek, knowing that's all it took to wipe away a frown. "You can make an exception for my wife this one time, can't you?"

"Don't try to be all sweet now. You know you should've told her." She shook Liam's arm off, and this time he laughed.

"This is thoughtful, dear, but come with me." She took the cake from Charlee. "We can eat together while I share some of the rules of the house. See that baker's rack over there?" She pointed to the tall, wide stand that had family photos on the top couple of shelves and four cakes, one bigger than the next, on the main shelf. "Those are all homemade. Can you cook?"

That was the last thing Liam heard of the conversation as his grandmother led his wife away.

"Well, Cuz. Seems like you've been busy," Nick said, as they began fixing their plates. "I'm starting to think I don't know you at all. Dating on the sly? Flying off to New York to get married?"

Liam and Charlee agreed to let people think what they wanted as far as how long they'd dated. Most of his family already knew that he was only going to tell them just so much anyway.

"What's next? You gon' tell us that you have a couple of kids running around?"

Liam shook his head. "That would be a no."

"Yeah, so you say," Nate added. He was holding one of his twin boys and juggling a plate in his other hand.

Jerry sidled up to them, his plate already loaded down. Since the family was growing and more people were attending the brunch, their grandmother set up additional food stations. Though the kitchen still held most of the food items, there were some in the dining room, as well as downstairs in the rec room where most of the men hung out.

"You're lucky Martina and Paul had to stop somewhere else first," Jerry said, biting into a meatball. "Otherwise, she probably would've acted a fool up in here. You know how she prides herself on knowing everybody's business before they're ready to share it. She's going to be pissed that she didn't know about this ahead of time."

"That's assuming she doesn't know," Jada said, handing a plate to Zack before she started preparing another one.

"She doesn't know, and I'm not worried. Charlee and I can handle Martina."

Chapter Twenty-Three

Charlee didn't think she had ever tasted food as good as what was on her plate. She'd heard of smothered fried chicken but had never tried it before. Now it was probably her favorite. Between that and the mac and cheese, fried cabbage, and the blacken fish, she didn't realize what she'd been missing. While there was plenty of soul food, there was also ample healthy choices, including a ton of vegetables and vegetarian dishes.

When Liam compared Sunday brunch to a brunch on steroids, he hadn't been exaggerating. She was so full. She didn't think she'd be able to eat for a week.

"I'm telling you. There is nothing wrong with getting married more than once," Liam's aunt Carolyn said. She was in her mid-fifties but looked as if she was Charlee's age. "Sometimes people don't get it right the first time."

"Or the second time," Katherine cracked, and giggles flowed around the long dining room table.

At first, it was just Charlee and Liam's grandmother, but they had since been joined by his mother, some of his cousins, and one of his aunts, Carolyn. Nick's wife, Sumeera and their youngest daughter, as well as Nate's wife, Liberty who was rocking one of her babies, was also at the table.

"Or the third time," Jada added, giggling with the others.

"Ha, ha, ha. I see you all have jokes," Carolyn said. "Okay, so I tried a few times. At least this third time I got it right."

"That's true. She definitely hit the jackpot with Lincoln," Christina, Jerry's younger sister, said. "He's fine and wealthy."

"A great combination if I must say so myself," Jada added.

They were definitely a lively group, bouncing from one topic to another. Rayne had told Charlee that some of the conversations got so heated that they had to ban certain subjects from being discussed during brunch. Like politics and who was the best cook in the family were off limits.

"Has anyone spoken to Toni this week?" Katherine Jenkins asked.

"I talked to her yesterday, and she mentioned that they had started adoption procedures." Christina glanced at Charlee. "Have you met Toni, yet?"

"I'm not sure. I met a few people at Rayne's baby shower, but—"

"She's the plumber," Rayne said.

"Oh, yeah." Charlee snapped her fingers. "She's the one who had on the bright orange T-shirt that said: *I'm the plumber who fixes the crap that you can't.*"

"Yep, that would be the one." Christina explained that Toni and her husband, Craig, had been trying to have a baby for years. She had gotten pregnant with their second child over a year ago, but had miscarried during her first trimester.

"She was devastated when she lost the baby," Jada added. Several of the cousins were pregnant at the same time, and Toni had stopped coming around as one baby was born after another.

Charlee's heart broke for the couple. She couldn't imagine that type of loss. She and Liam had talked about having kids in a year or two, which was fine by her. She wanted at least two, a boy and a girl, but first she wanted to enjoy her husband before they added to their family.

"What the hell?" Martina said, bursting into the dining room. "What is this nonsense I'm hearing about Liam being married? How in the heck did..." Her gaze landed on Charlee.

"MJ, don't come in starting no mess," Carolyn said. The resemblance between her and Martina was uncanny. Anyone would be able to tell they were mother and daughter or maybe even sisters.

Charlee set her fork down as Martina inched further into the room with her hands on her hips.

Once she was a few feet away, she narrowed her eyes at Charlee. "I just want to know. How'd you guys do it?" she asked, now folding her arms across her chest. "Nothing, and I mean *nothing* gets by me in this family. So I want to know what gives. How'd you guys pull this off without me even knowing you were dating?"

Liam was right. Martina was a trip...and Charlee liked her already.

"Apparently, some things do get by you," Jada said in a sing-song voice. "Let me formally introduce you to my new sister-in-law. MJ, this is Charlee. Charlee, this is our pain-in-the-butt cousin, Martina."

"Oh, I know Charlee. We've met once or twice. I just can't figure out how she and Liam got together. "Are you pregnant?"

"Uh, nooo," Charlee said, more amused than offended by the question.

"Did you get him drunk? That's it, isn't it? He was wasted, because there's no way he would just up and get married."

Charlee couldn't hold back the smile forcing its way through. "He was in his right mind when we said, I do."

Martina shook her head, frustration marring her face. She pulled out the only empty chair at the table and carried it to where Charlee and Katherine were sitting, sandwiching herself as close to the table as possible.

"I just need you to help me understand how this could've happened."

"Oh, give it a rest," Christina said from across the table. "You're just mad that they eloped without you knowing about it."

"Damn, right I'm mad!" Martina pounded the table.

"Martina!" Her grandmother swatted her arm. "What did I tell you about your mouth?"

"*Come on*, Gram. You more than anyone should understand what I'm going through right now. I usually know everything that goes on in this family, but now…" Her shoulders sagged and she shook her head. "Can't you see how upset I am?"

Charlee couldn't hold back the laugh that burst free, wondering how everyone could just sit there shaking their heads.

"I just can't with her." Katherine stood with her plate and headed to the door, but not before Charlee saw her fighting back a smile.

"I'm tellin' y'all." Jada said, pointing her fork at Martina. "Something is definitely wrong with this girl."

"Yep. She's crazy at its best," Christina added.

"Do you see what type of family you've married into?" Martina asked Charlee, her expression serious as she pointed to those at the table. "They think *I'm* the crazy one. You'll learn soon enough that the whole damn family is a little touched, especially those of you who married into this family."

Everyone burst out laughing, including Charlee. Rayne had told her plenty of stories about Sunday brunch, and more often than not, Charlee thought she'd been exaggerating. Apparently not. For the next twenty minutes, Martina kept up a running monologue. Sharing funny family stories one after another that had them all wiping tears from their eyes.

"Okay, who wants cake?" Katherine asked, carrying in slices of cake on a platter, everything from chocolate to coconut. She set the long, glass dish on the table where she was seated and immediately put two slices in front of Charlee. One was chocolate with chocolate frosting. The other was marble with chocolate frosting.

Charlee held back a groan. The marble cake was the one she had brought.

"Soo, Jada. Why didn't you warn your sister-in-law about what happens to people who don't bring home-cooked dishes to Sunday brunch?" Sumeera asked, a smile in her voice before she eyed Charlee.

"I would've had I known I had a sister-in-law."

Rayne leaned in close. "I told you not to bring anything," she said in a loud whisper.

Charlee eyed the cake. "I'm never going to live this down, am I?"

"Nope," several of them said.

Katherine reclaimed her seat and reached for a slice of caramel cake. "Okay, Charlee. Go ahead and eat. You don't have to announce which is better, because I already know. I just want you to recognize the difference."

Charlee ignored the laughing and took a bite of the marble cake which was amazing. She smiled to herself. She'd let them think that homemade is the way to go, even if what she brought was just as delicious.

Rayne nudged her with her elbow. "Don't get too pleased with yourself. Try the other one."

Charlee cut into the homemade one with her fork and put it in her mouth. *Oh, wow.* The cake was moist, decadent, and practically melted on her tongue. She had to keep from moaning, and there was no way she was going to look at anyone. She already felt their eyes on her.

"See, when you go against house rules, you have to pay the price," Martina said finishing off one slice of cake and reaching for another one. "We had to torture you with bought cake before you could taste one of these southern, down-home cakes."

"I can't believe you guys embarrassed her like this," Liberty said, rocking her baby who was now getting fussy.

"We did it to you. Now it's her turn," Martina explained. "We call this new ritual, welcome to the Jenkins family, sucka!"

Charlee couldn't remember the last time she laughed this hard or ate this much. When she finished the dessert, she stopped short of licking the fork. "If this is how you guys welcome people, I don't want to know what you do when you don't like someone."

"Oh please." Martina snorted. "We just run their asses up out of here!"

"Martina!" Katherine yelled, and a fit of laughter rocked the room.

Charlee's heart swelled as she glanced around at the Jenkins' women. Growing up, she had dreamed of having sisters and brothers, but it had been just her and her father. Though she had just met the Jenkins clan, she already loved them.

An hour later, she went in search of Liam and ran into him in the main hallway.

"Hey, baby. You doing all right?" he asked before kissing her.

"I'm great. I was just coming to look for you."

"Same here. We've been summoned to my grandfather's study."

"Both of us?"

He nodded.

Steven Jenkins had already congratulated them when they first made the announcement. Charlee wondered what he wanted.

They started walking, but Charlee slowed, taking in the tons of family photos that lined the walls of the long hallway. The picture that had caught her attention was the one with Liam, his brother Adam, Jada and her family and their parents.

"I guess we're going to have to take another photo now that you've joined the family," Liam said. It probably won't be for a while. Not until Adam gets home again."

"He's in the army, right?"

"Yes. He was in ROTC while in college before going full-duty into the military."

Charlee glanced at a couple of more photos before they continued on to the study. When they got to the door, Liam lifted his hand to knock but stopped when they heard Kingslee's voice.

"I didn't know your dad was here," he whispered, and started to knock again but Charlee stopped him with a hand on his arm when she realized they were talking about her.

"When I told my daughter that she'd only be considered for the CEO position if she was married, I had no idea she would actually go out and find a husband. And one of your grandsons at that."

Charlee's heart thudded against her rib cage, and she looked at her husband.

"Liam's not a leap before thinking kind of man," his grandfather said. "He wouldn't have married your daughter if he didn't love her. I saw them earlier, and he couldn't keep his eyes off of her."

"Yeah, I've seen them together, most recently at the office. I knew they'd had a history, but I didn't realize it was this serious. Still, I'm concerned that she only married him to get the position."

When the conversation went quiet, Liam backed away from her and the door.

"I can explain," Charlee hurried to say, her pulse pounding loudly in her ears as panic ricocheted through her. "Yes, he told me that the only way he'd give me the position is if I was married. I swear to you, that's not why I asked you. I love you so much. I didn't marry you for a job."

Her voice cracked, and her heart broke for fear that she was about to lose the best thing that ever happened to her.

Liam ran his hand over his mouth and down his chin, studying her. His dark eyes seemed darker and his expression was blank. She couldn't tell what he was thinking.

"Please, baby. You have to believe me." Tears welled in Charlee's eyes, but she batted them away. "I..."

The office door swung open, and Charlee and Liam turned.

"Oh, good. You're both here." Kingslee stood in the doorway not looking too pleased. "I hear congratulations are in order. Get in here," he said to Charlee, opening the door wider and barely sparing Liam a glance.

"I'm sorry, you guys," Mr. Jenkins said. "I didn't realize Kingslee didn't know."

"Yes. Imagine my surprise when I walked in here thinking I was invited over for dinner. Instead, I find out that my only daughter has run off and gotten married without me knowing that she was even dating."

"We wanted to tell everybody at the same time," Charlee said. "I planned to—"

"What? You actually planned something?" Kingslee asked, an edge to his voice.

Charlee felt Liam stiffen next to her, then his hand went to the small of her back. It was nice to know that even though he probably thought she married him under false pretenses, he was there with her.

"You know what, Dad? I understand if you're disappointed that we didn't tell you that—"

"Does you getting married all of a sudden have anything to do with the CEO position?"

"Of course not!"

Anger and hurt battled inside of Charlee. He was getting so good at embarrassing her. First, with Bradley, now with Mr. Jenkins.

"I would love to have the job that I have worked my butt off for, but I married Liam because I'm in love with him. I love that man more than I love breathing. So the fact that you think so little of me...that you think I'd use him or anyone like that, hurts. I get that you don't respect me, but—"

"That's enough, young lady. If you say that you—"

"It doesn't matter what I say. Good to know you think so little of me. I guess that's why you told my co-worker that I'm lonely. Was it out of pity that you tried to get him to date me?" She swiped at a few tears that fell, horrified that she was crying in front of them. Yet, she needed to tell him how she felt. "Is that the real reason you sent him to New York with me?"

"You know that's not true. I'm sorry I jumped to the wrong conclusion about you marrying Liam. After the conversation we had weeks ago about the CEO position, I had to ask. I wanted to make sure you didn't get married for the wrong reasons."

"Well, now you know. You'll have my letter of resignation on your desk in the morning." She turned abruptly and headed for the door, but Liam stopped her when his arm caught her around the waist.

"Hold up," he said quietly, pulling her against him and wiping tears from her face with the pad of his thumb. "Stop crying, okay?" The tenderness in his eyes almost made her cry harder, and Charlee didn't think she could ever love him more than she did in that moment. He could have easily believed that she had married him for the wrong reasons. He didn't. He trusted her, believed in their love for each other.

"Charlee," her father said. "Don't leave like this. I didn't mean to upset you."

"Actually, before we leave, there are some things that need to be straightened out," Liam said, his arm still around Charlee. "Mr. Kingslee, I've been in love with your daughter for a couple of years. Yes, we got married suddenly, but it wasn't without me being sure of my intentions. I overheard my grandfather telling you that I don't usually rush into anything. It's true. However, when you know you've found the right person, you go for it. Which I did."

He looked at Charlee, and she fell in love with him all over again. Considering their history, it meant everything that he believed she married him for love and not a job.

Kingslee's gaze bounced between her and Liam, while pride showed in Mr. Jenkins eyes. If only her father would look at her like that.

Charlee lowered her gaze. In all honesty, he did look at her like that most times. Deep down she knew he was proud of her accomplishments. He'd never been stingy with compliments and praised her often. Only recently, he had turned into a male chauvinist.

"One more thing," Liam continued. "Your daughter has sacrificed more for your company than you will ever know. Not considering her for the CEO position would be stupid."

"Liam," Mr. Jenkins said in a warning tone.

"Sorry, Pops. Let me rephrase that. Mr. Kingslee, don't count her out. She's a phenomenal woman who would be the best person for the job."

Her father nodded. "I'll take that under advisement." His attention landed on Charlee. "Sweetheart, before you resign, let's talk."

Emotion clogged her throat. Instead of saying anything, she nodded. Then she and Liam headed to the door.

"Well, Kingslee, I guess you have your answer." Steven Jenkins' voice carried to Charlee's ears. "Did I ever tell you about my granddaughter, Peyton, the one who took over Jenkins & Sons when I retired?"

He said more, but Charlee didn't catch the last of it as they walked out the door.

"Wait!" her father called out, rushing into the hallway. He reached for Charlee's hands. "I'm sorry if I hurt you. It wasn't my intent. I've always wanted what was best for you."

She wanted to be angry with him, but she couldn't. For so long it had been just the two of them, and she didn't want there to be animosity between them.

"Do you forgive me?"

"Yes." She hugged him. "I forgive you, and I'm sorry you didn't get to walk me down the aisle."

That had been something he had often talked about when she was growing up. He'd been looking forward to throwing her a big wedding and walking her down the aisle.

"Oh, no. There *will* be a wedding. Maybe not today or tomorrow, or even next month, but you're having a wedding." The words were spoken somewhat jokingly, but Charlee already knew that he would hound her until that day came.

She went back to Liam. "How do you feel about getting married again."

"I think I can deal with that, but do we have to invite my family?"

Charlee grinned and put her arms around his waist. "I love you."

He cupped her cheek, his mouth only inches from hers. "I love you, too. More than anything."

Chapter Twenty-Four

Charlee's fingers tapped away on the keyboard as she hurried to respond to an email that should've been taken care of days ago. As far as she was concerned, there was no such thing as catching up with work. Her to-do list grew faster than she could check items off.

The last month had been a whirlwind as she and Liam settled into married life. Their worlds had melded together almost seamlessly, and like she expected, he was the perfect husband.

My husband.

A wave of exhilaration pulsed through her veins at the thought of the man she vowed to spend the rest of her life with.

She stopped typing and glanced down at the sparkling wedding ring on her left hand. Shortly after they returned to Cincinnati, Liam had surprised her with a wedding band to go with the original engagement ring. The set was absolutely breathtaking. Even after a month, every few minutes she glanced at the symbol of their union, still amazed that they had gotten a second chance. She was finally married and not to just anyone, but married to the love of her life.

Even though it was still early in their marriage, she loved everything about being a wife. Even the cooking lessons she'd been receiving from Liam's mom and grandmother were fun. At least most of the time. Burning the noodles for the mac and cheese didn't go over well with his grandmother. And his mother was shocked the other Sunday when Charlee ruined the candied sweet potatoes. She had somehow gotten the sugar and salt amounts mixed up.

All in all, the lessons were going well, and Charlee planned to surprise Liam with a romantic dinner in the near future. For now, he insisted on handling their meals.

Emery gave a quick knock on the opened office door and rushed in. "The finest man who has ever stepped onto this floor is here to see you. Oh, and I'm not talking about your husband," she whispered.

Charlee grinned at Emery's comical expression. The same look seen on groupies when they spot their favorite singer. Her assistant had done an internship with the company all through college. After graduation, a year ago, Charlee offered her a permanent position. The young woman had more energy than three people put together. She was also extremely efficient with a wealth of knowledge, but it was times like this that reminded Charlee that she was so young.

"Okaay, so who is this person?"

"Mr. Garrison. He said you were expecting him, but I don't have him on your schedule. He's the new owner of Telecom Solutions."

"That's right. I forgot he was planning to stop by before heading back to Chicago. Sorry, I didn't mention it to you, but go ahead and show him in."

"Do you need me to hang out? Maybe take notes or answer any questions he might have? Or if you like, I can take him to dinner and—"

"Girl, get out of here and show him in."

"Will do," Emery said, grinning. "And for the record, I was just kidding."

"I know you were."

"Also, I'm heading downstairs to help Tiffany finish entering the rest of that data into the system. Do you want me to check back in before I leave for the day?"

Charlee glanced at her watch, noting that it was just after five. "No, that's all right. I'll be heading out in the next hour or two. Can you send the calls to voicemail before you leave?"

"No problem. Have a good evening, and I'll send Mr. Gorgeous, I mean Garrison in shortly."

When Emery walked out, Charlee stood and smoothed out her dress. She was looking forward to meeting the new owner who had purchased the telecom company that Fenlon had used for years. The old owners spoke highly of Garrison, who owned the business with his brothers. They were pleased that the new company had planned to keep the existing employees. No one lost their jobs.

That, along with what she'd researched on Garrison's company, was what encouraged Charlee to give them a try. So far, their services had been topnotch. Even though their main office was in Chicago, she never had a problem getting someone out within twenty-four hours.

"Hello. Ms. Fenlon?" A deep baritone sounded from the door and Charlee's head shot up.

Emery hadn't been kidding. The tall man with a low fade, a little scruff on his face, and a well-built body in a perfectly tailored suit could have easily graced a men's fashion magazine.

She hurried around her desk and met him as he moved further into the office. "It's Charlee, and you must be Mr. Garrison."

"Royce Garrison. It's nice to finally put a voice with a face." He shook her hand, and Charlee didn't miss the appreciative, full-body, inspection he gave her. "I had no idea you were this beautiful."

Her cheeks heated and she gave a small laugh, flattered by his words. Married or not, she'd be lying if she didn't admit that it was still nice to get a compliment from the opposite sex.

"Thank you. Come on in and have a seat. I'm glad we finally have a chance to meet." She walked around the desk and reclaimed her seat, then gestured for him to sit in one of the guest chairs facing the desk. "I also wanted to thank you for sending people out so fast last week."

"I'm glad we were able to accommodate you and your company." Royce set his laptop bag down and unbuttoned his suit jacket before sitting. "I trust that you were satisfied with the work."

"Definitely. I'm glad you were able to send Troy's team. They're the ones who originally installed the system."

As they discussed Fenlon's computer network, Charlee couldn't help but feel that she had seen Royce before. There was something so familiar about him, but she was sure they'd never met.

For the next twenty minutes, he told her about some of the additional services that they planned to offer their clients in the coming months. Most of what he told her was out of her realm of expertise, but she liked the new pricing system they were implementing.

"If you don't mind, I would love for you or one of the other owners, to meet with the head of our IT department. He would be better suited to answer some of your questions about our network needs. Do you have any plans on returning to Cincinnati anytime soon?"

He crossed one leg over the other but didn't break eye contact. "I didn't, but I think that could be arranged."

"Okay, I'll have someone from that office coordinate a date with you or your assistant in the next week or two." Charlee glanced at her schedule for the day. She needed to do one more thing before she could leave.

"My flight doesn't leave for a few hours. Are you available for dinner this evening? Maybe we could—"

"Sorry, but no." Charlee lifted her hand and wiggled her fingers, bringing attention to the wedding ring. "I can't."

Royce placed his hand over his heart, mock hurt covering his handsome features. "Ah, man. Somebody beat me to it?"

Charlee laughed but winced and reached behind her neck when her hair got caught in her necklace.

"What's wrong?"

"I remember why I usually have my hair up when I wear this necklace. My curls are caught in the clasp."

"Let me see if I can help."

Royce moved to the side of the desk, and Charlee gathered her hair, holding it up to give him better access to the necklace and strands that were caught.

"Wow, it's tangled pretty good."

He moved more behind her and gently tugged, his fingers grazing her skin. The tickle that shot down her spine had her thinking that this probably wasn't a good idea.

"You know what? Don't worry about it," she said, trying to move away, but he still had a hold on the necklace and her hair was still caught. "If I have to, I'll just cut it loose."

"Actually, I almost have it. Now, let's get back to the lucky guy who had sense enough to scoop you up. How long have you been married?"

"Thirty-three days."

Charlee's head jerked toward the door, and she winced again when her hair pulled. She was surprised to see Liam standing in the doorway holding a white paper bag. The name of her favorite restaurant was printed on the outside of it.

"Hey, baby," she said. "I didn't rea—"

"*Liam?*" Royce said from next to the desk, surprise in his tone. "What the hell are you doing here?"

"Why do you have your hands on my wife?"

"Your *wife*? You're married?"

"Wait. You two know each other?" Charlee was still trying to get her hair free as she slid her chair away from Royce and stood.

"Yeah, unfortunately." Liam set the bag on the table that was in front of the sofa and walked across the room to her.

His eyes that were intense and hard moments ago, suddenly held a tenderness when he looked at her. "What happen? What's wrong with your neck?"

"My hair is caught. Can you…"

He started working on the problem and within seconds had her unhooked. Then he turned to her guest. "Why are you here, Royce?"

*

The heavy weight of unease settled around Liam's shoulder as Royce slowly moved from the desk. Shock wasn't a strong enough word to describe what Liam felt when he walked in and saw his cousin. He might've known nothing was going on between him and Charlee, but flashes of the past rushed to the forefront of his mind. Every negative emotion that existed swirled inside of him at the sight of his wife being anywhere near the man.

"Can one of you answer my question?" Charlee asked. "How do you guys know each other?"

Liam slid an arm around her waist. "We're cousins."

Her eyes went big. "Cousins?"

"Yeah, I told you about him."

Royce folded his arms across his chest. "Oh, so you told her about what happened with the girl, huh?" The words were spat out in a way that made Liam wonder why the guy acted as if he was the victim.

"He mentioned the incident but didn't use your name. I didn't realize you were *that* cousin. Now that I see the two of you together, I can see the family resemblance."

Growing up, most people thought they were siblings. Liam even considered him a brother until that one Sunday afternoon that changed everything between them.

"Yeah, he's *that* cousin."

"Give it a rest, man. I was young and dumb back then. I can't believe you're still trippin' over BS that happened years ago."

Liam moved closer, anger boiling deep inside his gut. Royce still didn't get it. The fool still didn't understand what really happened that day. What he had destroyed.

"I'm not tripping over you screwing my college girlfriend," Liam ground out, barely hanging on to the control that had kept him from hunting his cousin down after so many years. "I'm tripping over the fact that you, my cousin, my best friend, my *family*, betrayed me. You disrespected me, as well as Gram and Pop's home."

Royce huffed out a breath. "Get over it. That happened a lifetime ago. Like you said, we're family. Sometimes we mess up. I don't know why I went after your girl. All I can say is that I'm sorry."

"You're stupider than I thought if all this time you thought this was about you sleeping with Jasmine. This ain't got shit to do with her. This is all about knowing my own blood would do something like that to me. Something so low and underhanded without thinking twice. *That's* my issue with you."

"I already told you I was sorry. What else do you want me to say?" His gaze went to Charlee, who was standing a short distance behind Liam. "Besides, you're married, and married to a *very* beautiful woman. I would think you could let that mess in the past go. Now, I could see if I was tryin' to push up on your wife. Then..."

Something snapped inside of Liam. He lunged forward before he could stop himself. Slamming his fist into his cousin's jaw, he put just enough power behind the punch to sting, but not enough to break anything.

"Liam!" Charlee screamed, grabbing his arm, probably thinking he was going to hit the bastard again.

Royce's head jerked and he staggered, barely keeping his balance. He braced himself against a nearby wall while he rubbed his jaw.

"Are you all right?" Charlee asked him, her hand still gripping Liam's arm.

"Yeah, I'm fine. I had it coming." Royce pushed away from the wall, still rubbing his jaw. "I see you still have a solid right hook, Cuz."

"Maybe you should go," Charlee told him.

"Yeah, that's probably a good idea, but first I owe you both an apology." Royce's eyes connected with Liam's. "I don't know how to fix what I broke between us, but I really am sorry. I know I messed up, and I'll understand if we can't go back to what we had."

Breathing hard, Liam struggled to control the anger still stirring within him. "We'll *never* be able to go back to what we had."

He nodded. "I know, and losing our bond is one of my biggest regrets. I also know 'I'm sorry' can't change what happened between us. I just hope over time you'll be able to forgive me."

Liam didn't respond. It would take a long time to trust his cousin again.

Royce grabbed his laptop bag and swung it over his shoulder. "Charlee, it was nice meeting you. Sorry about this. Hopefully, what happened here doesn't affect the working relationship between our companies."

"It doesn't, but going forward your contact person will be Bradley Handler. I'll make sure I pass your information and what we discussed on to him."

Royce nodded, and Liam kept quiet. He never wanted to do anything to hinder her job or work environment. Even though he trusted her completely, he was glad she wouldn't be dealing with Royce.

Once his cousin was gone, Liam closed the door and locked it. He turned to his wife. The softness of her eyes did him in each time he looked at her. He never knew he was capable of loving someone as much as he loved this woman.

"I am so sorry," he said. "I came to surprise you with dinner just in case you were working late. I had no intention of barging in here and messing up your meeting."

"It's all good." She gripped the front of his Henley and tugged hard enough to bring their faces within inches from each other. "I'm just glad to see you."

Before Liam could respond, her mouth covered his and all thoughts of dinner and Royce flew from his mind. She kissed him with a passion that left no doubt that she loved him as much as he loved her.

When he stopped by, he hadn't planned on christening her office, but the urgency of her kiss sent heat charging to every cell in his body. His need to be buried deep inside of her grew with every lap of her tongue, exploring the inner recesses of his mouth. And when she ground her softness against his hard shaft, he knew they wanted the same thing.

"You know when you rub up against me like this, it's game on," he murmured against her lips then broke off the kiss. Breathing hard, his lips went to her neck, nibbling on her soft, scented skin. "I want you so bad. Right here. Right now. So if you're expecting more visitors, stop me now."

"No visitors. No stopping."

Liam backed her to the wall. This was one of those times when he was glad that she had on her way-too-tall, high heels. Their bodies aligned perfectly with the extra height the shoes provided.

Charlee hiked up her dress, revealing the skimpiest panties he'd ever seen on her, and his thoughts jumbled. Need spread through him quicker than an uncontrollable forest wildfire.

"Damn, you look good." He glided his hands slowly up the side of her thighs, finding pleasure in the way she shivered under his touch. "Let's get you out of these," he said.

He began sliding the tiny strip of nothing over her hips, and his shaft grew harder, throbbing with need as he glided the material down her shapely legs. He stood in awe of her incredible body, bare before him, as he stuffed the panties into the front pocket of his jeans. He couldn't take his eyes off of her.

"You are truly one sexy woman."

She gave him a shy smile but then it turned wicked, mischief sparkling in her big brown eyes.

"Your turn," she said, still holding up her dress. "Let me see what I *know* you're working with."

He chuckled, quickly unfastening his pants to free himself. "I can do better than showing you. How about I let you feel what I'm working with."

"Liam!" she gasped when he lifted her off the floor. Her arms went around his neck, and she wrapped her legs around his waist. He braced her against the wall for extra support as they stared into each other's eyes.

"You know I love this position."

"I know." His lips met hers and he devoured her mouth as he slid into her sweet heat, marveling at the way her inner muscles contracted around him. She felt so good.

And wet, and hot, and tight, he thought as he moved inside of her. It didn't matter how many times or how many ways they made love, he didn't think he would ever get enough of her. Each time was just as amazing as the first time.

It didn't take long before they both were panting as he pumped in and out of her with more force, going a little deeper with each thrust. The erotic moans she made, spurred him on, causing him to move faster and harder. What Liam didn't want to do was bruise her back as it rubbed against the wall, but he couldn't stop.

His heart was practically pounding out of his chest as his release neared. With her unsteady breathing and the jerkiness of her body, it was safe to say that she was almost at that point, too.

"Liam…" Charlee whimpered. She tightened around him. "I—I… Oh yes, right there. Ri—"

She moaned, and her body shook violently against him, making it hard to hold her up. But he held firm, pumping into her like a man possessed until his body stiffened. A growl rumbled in his throat and his release plowed through him like an out of control locomotive pushing him over a cliff.

He wobbled on unsteady legs and pressed Charlee firmly against the wall, ensuring that they didn't collapse to the floor. While he fought to get air into his lungs, he slowly set her on her feet but didn't remove his arm from around her.

She laid her forehead on his shoulder. "That was…"

"Intense," he said, still breathing hard. "I'm glad you're the boss."

"Why?"

"Because you have a bathroom in this big ass office."

She released a tired laughed. "I've been trying to figure out the advantages of being the boss. Now I know."

"How about we get cleaned up and get out of here."

She lifted her head and kissed him sweetly. "That's the best idea I've heard all day."

Chapter Twenty-Five

Liam is going to kill me.

The last thing Charlee wanted to do was miss their date, but she was already three hours late. Not just any date. They were celebrating their three-month anniversary.

She should've been home with her man. Instead, she was still at the office.

"Oh good. You're still here," Bradley said as he strolled in carrying a manila folder.

The whole day had been one disaster after another. The worst being that there had been an accident at a job site in Detroit and one of their cranes was at the center of the investigation. This was the first time that she could remember, that a crane had snapped at the boom point. In this case, it had damaged not only the building the client's company was working on, but thousands of dollars' worth of material had been destroyed.

OSHA, the Occupational Safety and Health Administration, was investigating the incident, but Charlee also wanted her own investigation done. She had already contacted their lawyer and a private investigator.

"We need to go over—"

"Bradley, I have to get home. Whatever else you need to discuss with me will have to wait until Monday."

Charlee scooped up her cell phone from the desk and slid it into the side pocket of her oversized Chanel bag. The files that she still hadn't had a chance to review also went into the bag.

"Charlee, this is important. It'll only take a minute."

"I'm leaving."

She had let him impose on her time too often over the last few weeks. There'd been presentations, new contracts, and a new employment program that they'd implemented.

But not tonight. Tonight, she had to hurry home to her husband with hopes that he hadn't finally given up on her.

For over the past month, she'd been getting home later and later. At first, Liam hadn't complained. He often brought her dinner. Stopped by during lunch, insisting that she take a break. There had even been one late night that he brought his work to her office and stayed there with her, not wanting her to drive home alone so late at night.

Now that was love.

How'd she pay him back? She started working even longer hours.

"This can't continue," she said, more to herself, but didn't care that Bradley heard her. "This is the last week that I'll be staying in the office this late."

"Okay, but right now, we have to discuss the marketing plan for the new tractors we're rolling out in a few months. I know you wanted to let Diane take lead on that project, but I don't think she can handle the work."

Charlee stood and double checked the top of her desk, making sure she had everything she needed to work from home during the weekend.

She looked at her co-worker. "Whatever you want to discuss, including Diane's project, will have to wait until Monday. I'm out of here."

"Come on, Charlee. Whatever you're rushing off to can wait, but this," he held up the manila folder, "can't."

"Let's go. I need to lock up my office. If you want, you can fill me in on the way to the parking garage. That's all the time I can give you."

He huffed out a breath and followed her into the hallway, waiting for her to lock the door.

"Clearly, your priorities are out of whack," he grumbled, keeping up with her as she hurried to the elevator. "How do you expect to be CEO when the business doesn't come first? You're going to throw everything you've worked for away for a man?"

Charlee rounded on him, getting in his face. "I'm going to say this one time. So you'd better listen good. My personal life is none of your business, but for the record, Liam is not just a man. He's my husband, and I'd give up *everything* for him."

"Charlee, I didn't mean to—"

"And *when* I become CEO, you'd better make sure you can do your job. Coming to me for everything or to the person who will fill my current role is not gonna fly. Some of these issues you claim are super important, *you* should be able to take care of. So, whatever is in that file folder you're holding, handle it. I'll see you Monday morning."

Twenty minutes later, she pulled into her garage, cringing at the fact that it was almost ten o'clock. Way past the time they were supposed to have a nice, romantic dinner.

"I have to do better," she grumbled, grabbing her things out of the car.

Liam had called her twice. Once earlier just to hear her voice, and again around five to confirm that she'd be home by six-thirty. She'd had every intention of getting home early. When she texted him a couple of hours ago, explaining that she'd be a little late, he'd been okay with it. Telling her that he was looking forward to spending the evening with her. But when she texted him an hour ago, she hadn't heard back.

No doubt he was pissed. At some point, he was going to quit trying to make their marriage work. She had recently postponed their wedding, claiming she didn't have time. Liam was understanding but did express concern that the wedding would never happen if she couldn't make time to help with the planning.

Charlee huffed out a breath, frustrated with herself. She walked into the house, leaving her bag and jacket in the mudroom. When she entered the kitchen and dining room area, the lights were dimmed. Candles, that looked as if they'd been burning a while, graced every available flat surface. A beautiful bouquet of pink roses sat in the center of the dining room table that was set for two.

Guilt pierced her chest. How could she have messed this night up, especially knowing how much they both were looking forward to it? Some of the work she'd done earlier, could've been passed on to someone else. Yet, she had insisted on doing it herself. Now, she'd have to pay the cost for not delegating.

A jazz melody flowed through the surround sound. Seeing that Liam listened to music by ThaSaint practically every night, Charlee recognized the tune immediately. *The Way I Feel For You* played softly, making her feel even worse about being late.

God, he really is going to kill me.

"Liam?" she called out, and pulled up short when she reached the living room.

He was sitting on the sofa, his feet propped up on the coffee table and a glass with dark liquid in his hand. He looked the epitome of calm, but she knew better. Only those who knew the brooding man would notice his simmering anger.

"Where've you been?" he asked, his words surprisingly slurred.

"At work." She slowly approached him, knowing a simple sorry wouldn't make up for ruining their evening. "I miss calculated how long it would take me to finish up today, and then Bradley came to—"

"Don't mention that asshole's name in my house," he snarled.

Charlee clamped her lips shut. He didn't like Bradley much, especially when her co-worker called the house on Sunday mornings to discuss work. Tonight, though, this was all on her. She was the one who had screwed up. Her husband had every right to be upset. He had been nothing but patient for months, planning their time together around her crazy work schedule. All he had asked was for her to commit to a date night during the week, and that they spend some time together on the weekend. Yet, she struggled to do either. It wasn't because she couldn't. Her priorities were out of whack just as Bradley accused, but not the way he meant.

Something had to change. She had to start delegating more or risk losing everything that was important to her. Just the thought sent panic racing through her body. She couldn't lose Liam. She couldn't let the man she absolutely adored walk out of her life again.

Not this time. Not ever.

Liam tossed back the rest of his drink. Then slammed the glass on the side table.

Oh, no. This is not good, Charlee thought when she noticed the half-empty bottle of bourbon.

Her husband was a casual drinker. A beer once or twice a week, but rarely did he indulge in hard liquor unless he was playing poker or watching a game with some of his cousins. Apparently, he also drank when he was pissed.

Charlee's pulse thumped loudly in her ears as she tried to think of some way of salvaging the evening.

"Liam, if you haven't eaten already, we can still—"

"I—I'm not do—doing this anymore." His voice was a low rumble, the agony behind his words cut through Charlee like a shard of glass.

"Baby, I'm sorry. I know I've been messing up our plans lately, but I promise, going forward—"

"No. I've heard it t-too many ti—times." He stood on wobbly legs, tilting to his left and Charlee rushed to him.

"Let me help you."

He jerked away, stumbling into a side table, but righting himself. "Don't touch me. Ge-get your bags." He drunkenly lifted his arm and pointed to a couple of pieces of her luggage that were near the front door. "And ge—get out of my hou—house."

When he headed toward the hallway that led to their bedroom, panic crawled down Charlee's spine. Then within seconds it was replaced with annoyance.

"I get that you're mad, but I'm not leaving!" she shouted. "This is my house, too, and I'm not going anywhere! Let's just talk about this."

"I'm done tal—talking." He kept walking until he disappeared down the hall.

Charlee's chest tightened. She messed up again, and this time she didn't know how to fix it.

What she did know was that if she left that house, there would be no coming back. He wouldn't give her a third chance.

No way am I leaving.

She blew out the candles that were still lit in the dining and living rooms and put away the food. Once that was done, she shut off the music.

Kicking off her shoes and curling up on the sofa, she made herself comfortable.

It's going to be a long night.

*

The next morning, Liam slowly lifted his heavy eyelids, blinking several times to push through the dense fog of sleep. Why did it feel as if there was drilling going on in his head? Without getting up, he glanced around. A sliver of light from above the closed curtains, cast just enough illumination to the otherwise dark bedroom, letting him know that it was a new day.

What a night. Bits and pieces of the night before floated through his mind.

No more hard liquor.

While waiting for his wife to get home, he had gone through all types of emotions. Excitement. Frustration. Disappointment. Anger. He couldn't remember if they were in that exact order, but he was pretty sure those feelings had been on rotation inside of him. At least until he started drinking. After the third or fourth glass of bourbon, he just didn't give a damn.

Now he felt like crap. Since his mind was awake and he was thinking hard, the excruciating pounding inside of his head was getting worse. His mouth felt as if it was stuffed with cotton balls, and his body throbbed. More than all of that, his heart ached at how he had treated Charlee.

Get out of my house.

It didn't matter how angry he'd been, he couldn't believe he had said those words to his wife. Unfortunately, mostly everything after that was a blur. He didn't even remember getting into bed. What he did remember was how tired he was of trying to make their marriage work. Tired of being the only one to put forth an effort.

Something had to change because divorce wasn't an option. He loved her too much to live the rest of his life without her.

A wave of concern pulsed through his body. "I gotta go find my wife."

He wasn't sure where she would've gone that time of night, especially since they had rented out her condo. She wouldn't have gone to her father's house or Jerry and Rayne's place. They had vowed that no matter what, they would always keep others out of their marriage. That meant if they had problems, they would work together to figure them out, not pull others into their issues.

He closed his eyes and pinched the bridge of his nose. Where would she have gone? Wherever she was, he'd find her. First, he had to do something about his pounding headache and the awful taste in his mouth. Glancing down, he realized he hadn't even gotten undressed.

He lifted his head a few inches off the pillow, but the hammering inside of it forced him to lay back down.

Definitely. No more hard liquor.

He glanced at the clock. *Ten o'clock.* Liam couldn't recall the last time he'd slept that late.

He slowly sat up and swung his legs over the edge of the bed and froze. Laying on a makeshift pallet of blankets and pillows on the floor next to the bed was his wife. The covers had been kicked off and she was curled into a fetal position. Her wild curls hid part of her face as her head rested at an odd angle on the pillow. Dressed in one of his T-shirts, the cotton had ridden up to her waist, revealing tiny pink panties.

Liam hadn't heard her before, but now her soft snores reached his ears.

Relief flooded his body at the sight of her, but guilt gnawed on his nerves. He was glad she hadn't left, but he hated seeing her laying on the floor. Why hadn't she just gotten into the bed? It couldn't have been that she was afraid he'd kick her out of it. He hadn't even heard her enter the room. She even could've slept in the guest room.

Careful not to step on her, he clambered out of bed. An overwhelming feeling of protectiveness descended on him when he lifted her off the floor. Mad or not, going forward he had to take care of her. They couldn't have a repeat of the night before.

He laid her on the bed and stared down at her. A suffocating sensation clawed up his chest and tightened inside his throat. Had she done what he asked, he could've lost her for good. That thought left a hollowness within him. He didn't even want to imagine a life without her again.

We're going to figure this out, he thought and headed to the bathroom. He took a couple of ibuprofens, showered, and climbed back into bed; glad it was Saturday. He didn't know if Charlee had to be at work, but he had no intention of waking her.

Liam pulled her against the front of his body. Having her right where she belonged, his eyes drifted closed, and he fell into a deep sleep.

Chapter Twenty-Six

When Charlee entered the kitchen, Liam was sitting at the table with a coffee mug in one hand and his cell phone in the other.

"Good morning," she said, hoping he wasn't still angry with her.

He glanced up and gave her a quick once over. "Morning." He went back to reading something on his phone.

She wasn't sure if he was trying to finish what he'd been doing, or if this was his way of ignoring her. Either way, there was no way around this wedge between them. They had to talk.

She tightened the sash of her silk robe before sitting across from him. "Liam, I—"

"Are you hungry?" He was already rising out of his seat before she could answer.

Charlee sighed. He wasn't going to make this easy. "A little."

"Just a little? It doesn't look like you ate anything last night." He moved around the kitchen, pulling a box of grits out of the pantry and other items from the refrigerator.

"After ruining our evening, I didn't deserve to eat last night."

Whatever else he was about to pull out of the refrigerator, he stopped and looked at her. "Babe, don't—"

"It's true. I will never be able to apologize enough for the way I've been treating you," she choked out, batting away tears that suddenly filled her eyes. "I feel awful, and I'm so sorry."

His slow gait carried him across the kitchen to where she sat.

"C'mere." He tugged on her hand, pulling her out of the seat. When he opened his arms to her, she went willingly.

This time Charlee couldn't stop the tears. For much of the night, she feared that things were over between them. That he wouldn't forgive her. She shuddered at the thought that she could've lost him for good. The same way she had before.

His hold on her tightened, and he kissed the side of her head. "I hate it when you cry."

"And I hate disappointing you."

It seemed that all wasn't lost. Considering he was there, holding her, and was about to prepare something to eat, meant he hadn't given up on her completely. She wanted to vow never to hurt him again, but what if it turned out to be more empty promises? What if she never learned how to juggle her marriage and her career?

"Once I fix you something to eat, then we can talk," Liam said, rubbing her back. After a few minutes, he loosened his hold. "Give me about fifteen or twenty minutes. Any special requests?"

Charlee wiped her face. "No. Whatever you make will be fine. I'll go and get dressed."

While showering, Charlee thought about what she'd say to him. Short of quitting her job, what could she do to prove that he was the most important person in her life? She already knew delegating some of her work was vital, but what would it take to keep that going? The first month of their marriage, they had gotten into a nice rhythm. Most days she arrived home between seven-thirty and eight, but on date nights, she pulled in around six-thirty, determined to abide by their original agreement.

How could she recommit to their agreement and maintain it?

A short while later, the smell of bacon and something sweet like cinnamon rolls, lured her back into the kitchen.

"It smells wonderful in here." She eyed the sweet treat on the counter, next to the bacon and eggs. "You were able to make cinnamon rolls that fast?"

"Nah, Gram made them for you yesterday," he said of his grandmother. "I went by and picked them up before dinner."

A twinge of guilt crept back in, but Charlee pushed it down as she fixed her plate. Neither of them spoke until they carried their food to the table.

"I owe you an apology," Liam started. "It didn't matter how disappointed I was, I shouldn't have ever asked you to leave. That was out of order, and I'm glad you stayed."

Charlee nodded but didn't look at him. Shame consumed her. Here she had this amazing man who loved her unconditionally, cooked for her, and made her feel special, and she almost threw it all away.

She bit her bottom lip before finally meeting his gaze. "I couldn't leave. I know I keep screwing up, but I just couldn't leave. I love you. I know I have a funny way of showing it, but you're my everything, Liam. I don't want to walk through life without you."

He wiped his mouth with a napkin and covered her hand with his. "I feel the same way. I just don't know what else to do. Your career is important to you. I get that, and I want you to be happy. I also want our relationship to continue to grow stronger. That's not going to happen if we don't spend time together."

She turned her hand over and squeezed his. "I don't want you to think this is yet another empty promise, but you have my word that there will be changes, starting today."

"If you're thinking about quitting your job, don't. That can't be one of the options. You love what you do."

"I love you more. I don't want to quit, but I want you to know that I will if it means keeping you."

"We have to come up with another way." They went back to eating. "Am I being unreasonable?"

"You haven't been unreasonable about anything. Putting in twelve to fifteen-hour days, six days a week is ridiculous. I know that. It's just sometimes I get caught up, but not anymore. Whether I become CEO or not, my work hours are not going to exceed ten-hour days during the week. As for the weekend, unless it's an emergency, I won't be going into the office."

"Wait. Of course, I'd love to have you home early. What I don't want is for you to start putting restrictions on yourself that you might not be able to uphold. Let's start first with going back to our original agreement. Wednesday date nights, and we spend Sunday or at least part of Sunday together."

"Okay." Even though she was serious about getting strict with her hours, her response sounded unconvincing to her own ears. She was pretty sure Liam had picked up on it, too.

He searched her eyes as if they would tell him what he needed to know. "If that's not what you want, tell me."

"I want every night with you. I'm just afraid I'm going to mess up again."

"You won't. We're in this together. We'll get it right. Even if it takes the rest of our lives."

Charlee smiled for the first time that day. "I'm looking forward to spending the rest of my life with you. Thank you for not giving up on me," she whispered, getting choked up by the words.

"What do you want to do about the wedding?" he asked. "Do you still want a formal ceremony?"

"I do. Your grandmother mentioned that we might be able to use the church that she and your grandfather attend. Would you be okay with getting married in November, before Thanksgiving?"

"I'll marry you again anytime, but that's less than a month away. Can we pull everything together by then?"

"I think so. Jada and Rayne agreed to help with anything we need. If we can't get the church, your grandmother mentioned that we could use their ballroom."

"But you wanted a church wedding."

"I know." Charlee had been blown away by the size and the elegance of his grandparents' ballroom, but she had envisioned getting married in a church. Since she was already married, it really wasn't as big of a deal. "It's not that serious," she finally said.

"Yeah, it is. I want you to have what you want. I'll find another church if it doesn't work out with Gram's." He sat back in his seat and folded his arms across his chest, studying her. "What else? What do you need from me to ensure that we stay together forever?"

Charlee rubbed the back of her neck, trying to work out the stiffness. There was something else she wanted. She just hadn't planned on bringing it up yet.

"Tell me," he said as if reading her mind.

"When you told me to get out of your house..." She broke eye contact, struggling to tell him how she felt without getting emotional. "You hurt me."

She stood abruptly with her almost empty plate, prepared to take it to the sink. He stopped her, his arm blocking her path. Pulling her back toward him, he took the plate from her hands and sat it back on the table. Then he pulled her onto his lap.

"Sweetheart, I am so sorry. I never want to do anything to hurt you. Last night, I'll admit I was disappointed and drinking didn't help matters." He held her closer and placed a lingering kiss on her cheek. "You have my word that I'll never say that to you again. I hope you can forgive me."

Charlee cupped his cheek, glad they were having this time together. "Of course, I forgive you."

"But?"

She shook her head. He was too perceptive.

"But I want us to move. I want us to buy a house together before the end of the year."

He nodded, looking deep in thought. "All right. I'll call Sumeera," he said of Nick's wife who was a real estate agent. "Do you already know what you want in a house?"

"Yes, but before we discuss the house in detail, I want us to kiss and make up."

That sexy grin that always made her all tingly inside made an appearance.

"I think I can handle kissing and making up." He brushed his mouth over hers, but then turned serious. "I hope you know how much I love you."

"I do, and I want you to know that I'm crazy in love with you. I don't like it when we fight."

"Yeah, me either." He touched his forehead to hers. "No more getting drunk and going to bed mad."

"Good. Now, can we kiss and make up?"

"Anything you want, baby."

He captured her mouth and kissed her with a passion that left no doubt about his feelings for her. She was the luckiest woman alive, and couldn't wait to marry him again.

Epilogue

One month later...

"Okay, you have something old, the pearls that Gram gave you to wear. Something new is your wedding dress. You have something blue, the garter belt," Rayne said, ticking off the items on her fingers.

Charlee wasn't a traditional person and didn't really believe that she needed something old, something new and all the other stuff. All she wanted was to marry her husband again. This time in front of their family and friends.

Well, most of their family.

Pain squeezed her heart, and an emptiness she'd felt earlier in the week settled around her. There had definitely been one advantage to eloping. When she and Liam married in New York, it was all about them. All about starting their lives together. Just the two of them.

With a wedding, there were so many moving parts. So many people playing various roles, whether helping secure a location, or assisting with decorations. As they started making plans, Charlee realized her mother wouldn't be there to help shop for a wedding dress. She wouldn't be there to fuss over all the small details of the wedding and the reception. She also wouldn't be there to give last minute advice.

"I know you miss your mom," Rayne said, sitting on the pink settee next to Charlee.

They were in a small room in the church that Liam's grandmother, Gram, had dubbed the bridal suite.

"I wanted to give you that something borrowed." Rayne pulled a familiar looking silver pouch from her purse, and Charlee smiled through the tears she'd been trying to hold back. "I'm going to let you borrow the friendship locket that you gave me before you moved to Cincinnati. We can wrap it around the stems of your bouquet."

Charlee accepted the dainty jewelry, the locket dangling from a silver chain. The locket had been too small to inscribe a message inside, but on the back read: *Friends are just like family*.

"I can't believe you still have this." She recalled the day she gave it to Rayne.

They had attended a couple of years of high school together. Growing up, their lives couldn't have been more different. Charlee had parents who adored her and could give her anything she wanted, while Rayne had grown up in foster care. She had bounced from one home to the next until she was in high school, then she lived in a group home.

Their differences actually bonded them most. It wasn't until Charlee lost her mother, did their similarities come to the forefront.

"After your mom died, and I found out you were moving to Cincinnati with Kingslee, I think I cried for a week," Rayne said, grabbing the box of tissue that sat on the table in front of them. She snatched out a few sheets and handed some to Charlee.

"Yeah, those weeks that followed felt like the end of the world. Remember how I begged my dad to take you with us?"

Rayne smiled. "I do, and I loved you even more then. I never felt wanted, but the way you pitched a fit when your father told you that it wasn't that easy to take a minor out of town, made me feel as if you couldn't live…" Rayne visibly swallowed, her tears causing more to leak from Charlee's eyes. "You made me feel as if you couldn't live without me. You'll never know what that meant to me. You were the first person to make me feel wanted."

"Oh, Rayne." Charlee squeezed her friend's hand. She had no idea she felt that way.

"There were days your gift was the only hope I had to hang on to. So today, I'm loaning it to you. Not as just something borrowed, but also to symbolize the happiness that you've brought me over the years."

"Is that what *something borrowed* represents?"

Rayne's brows furrowed. "Um, I think. Girl, I don't know for sure. Just go with it."

They both laughed, and the heaviness Charlee had felt moments ago lifted. Her mother might not be there physically, but she would live in Charlee's heart forever.

"It's a good thing we got here early, and Jada hasn't done my makeup," she said, drying her eyes.

"I know, right? She would kill us both. Me for making you cry and you for messing up your makeup."

"But seriously," Charlee started. "Thank you for the *something borrowed*, and for being here for me."

"Of course, I'd be here. You saved my life. I don't know what I would've done had you not convinced me to move to Cincinnati."

"You're a survivor, Rayne. I just helped a little. You're the one who didn't give up."

"Actually, I gave up more times than not, but that's another story. Look at us. We're married to amazing men, have great lives, and we're a part of a big, crazy family."

They laughed again, and even harder when they started talking about Martina's shenanigans at the rehearsal dinner the night before. She was good at getting everyone riled up, causing arguments that lasted longer than necessary. All in all, the night had turned into a fun celebration. The Jenkins family was like no other, and Charlee was so grateful to be one of them now.

She hugged Rayne. "I love you, girl. Thank you for being my friend."

Her heart overflowed with love for the people in her life. Yes, she missed her mother, and no one could ever replace her, but Liam and his family had given her more than she could've ever hope for.

Forty-five minutes later, Charlee stood in front of the full-length mirror, admiring Jada's handy work. The form-fitting, strapless gown that she had designed with a lace overlay, beading and sequins was absolutely exquisite.

"Wow, you're beautiful, sweetheart," her father said from the doorway.

Charlee turned to him smiling. Her heart was so full she felt as if she would burst.

"You're looking pretty handsome yourself. I guess it's time, huh?"

"It is, but I wanted to talk to you for a minute."

"Dad, please don't make me cry again."

"I won't. I promise." He moved further into the room and kissed her cheek.

Over breakfast that morning, they'd had a heart to heart. By the time he finished telling her how much he loved her and how proud he was of her, Charlee had been an emotional wreck. It was just the two of them for so long. She hadn't realized how much her marriage had affected him. He was crazy about Liam and thought he was perfect for her, but now he had to share her. For him, that was taking some getting used to.

"How do you think your husband will feel being married to a CEO?"

Charlee's eyes rounded and she brought her hands to her mouth, but stop short of messing up her lipstick. A giggle bubbled inside of her. "Oh, my goodness. Does that mean what I think it means?"

"It means that I will officially retire at the end of the year. The job is yours if you want it."

"Yes!" She did a fist pump, making her father laugh. "Of course, I want it! Liam is going to flip."

Since finding out she was up for the position, he'd been bringing the possibility up in conversation at every turn. Even when they found the perfect house in Indian Hill, a suburb of Cincinnati, he ruled it out because it was too far from her office. Claiming that as the CEO, her hours might be longer. He didn't want her driving that far alone at night.

She loved him for thinking of her, but had explained that the hours she currently worked, were probably longer than she'd work as CEO. In the end, they put in an offer on the house she wanted and got it. They agreed to figure out the commute if she got the job.

"I can't believe it. I'm going to be the CEO." She said it over and over again. Her excitement growing as it sunk in. "Thank you. It means everything that you trust me enough to run the company that you built."

"The company *we* built. I couldn't have done it without you. You're going to be an awesome CEO."

Charlee put her hand on her chest. "Aw, Dad. Thank you. Thank you for all you've done for me. I love you so much."

"I love you more, baby girl."

"All right, you guys. It's time," Rayne said as she and Jada strolled into the room, looking gorgeous in their sky-blue gowns.

"Well, do you approve?" Charlee asked as Jada walked around her, giving her another once over.

"Yep, I approve. You look amazing."

Kingslee offered Charlee his arm. "Now, let's get you married."

*

Liam stepped into the sanctuary with Jerry, his best man, and some of their cousins who were groomsmen. As they got into position a wave of excitement course through his body.

He couldn't wait to see his wife. The night before had been hell. It was the first time that he and his wife had been apart since before running into each other in New York.

All because of his mother. She insisted on Charlee staying at their house. Claiming it was bad luck for him to see the bride before the wedding. She didn't seem to care that they'd been married for four months.

Liam glanced out at the audience, not surprised that the sanctuary was full with mostly family and just a few friends.

"You ready for this?" Jerry asked, gripping Liam's shoulder.

"You do realize that I'm already married to her, right?" Liam asked, finding it a little amusing that all morning, people had been asking him if he was ready.

"Yeah, you're talking all tough now. Wait until you see her walking down the aisle. It will feel as if you're seeing her for the first time."

"If you say so."

A few minutes later, music started playing and the vocalist started singing Anthony Hamilton's, *The Point Of It All*. Liam waited anxiously as the bridesmaids walked down the aisle and took their places, but it was Stormy and her vibrant personality that stole the show. He had never met a kid who could light up a room the way she could, and when she blew Jerry a kiss, she captured the hearts of everyone in the audience.

Now Liam just wanted to see his wife. After their last month, he and Charlee had done more than kiss and made up. Their relationship was thriving. They were both giving a hundred percent, and he couldn't be happier. He fell in love with his amazing woman more and more every day.

When the music switched over to Ruelle's, *I Get To Love You*, Liam released a slow calming breath, willing himself to calm down. Instead of the traditional wedding march, Charlee had chosen this song to walk in on.

Where is she? It seemed to take forever for her and her father to make an appearance. A sudden bout of anxiety pumped through Liam's veins, and he rubbed his hands together.

Why was he nervous? They were already married.

"And it begins," Jerry cracked, humor lacing his words.

Seconds later, Charlee appeared in the wide doorway with her father. Liam's knees went weak. His heart galloped, and his breath caught at the sight of his wife.

Good Lord.

Jerry chuckled next to him as if knowing what he was thinking.

Wait. Did I say that out loud?

"I told you it would feel like the first time. So let me know if you're going to pass out. I'll try to catch you before you hit the floor."

"Man, shut up," Liam mumbled, unable to pull his gaze from Charlee. She was without a doubt, the most beautiful woman he had ever laid eyes on. More importantly, she was his.

Once she and her father were next to him, Kingslee shook Liam's hand. "Take care of my baby," he said, his voice gruff with emotion.

"I will. *Always.*"

Liam reached for Charlee and the moment they touched, an electric current shot up his arm. It reminded him of the first time they'd met years ago in her father's office. The same thing had happened when she shook his hand. Now here they were about to become husband and wife...again.

He searched her eyes, looking for any sign that she wasn't all right. Then his gaze traveled the length of her shapely body, looking mouth-watering tempting in her dress.

"Wow." The word slipped out before he could rein it in.

She grinned and leaned in a little closer, her signature scent settling around him. "So, we're back to one-word responses from you, huh?"

Liam laughed, unable to help himself. This woman had crashed into his life, twisted it upside down, and made him the happiest man on this side of heaven. He didn't know what their future held, but he knew that it would be full of laughter, love, and adventure.

For the next few minutes, he struggled to listen as the officiant performed a traditional ceremony. He perked up when they finally got to the part he'd been looking forward to.

"You may now kiss your bride."

"Gladly." Liam wrapped Charlee in his arms and kissed her as if he hadn't seen her in years instead of hours. There were days he still couldn't believe that she was his. That he was hers. That they had found their way back to each other. Maybe she'd been right. Maybe fate had played a hand in bringing them together. Whatever the case, he was grateful for their second chance.

When they finally came up for air, the minister said, "Ladies and gentlemen, I present to you, Mr. and Mrs. Liam Jenkins."

As the room roared with cheers and clapping, Liam kissed his wife again. He couldn't get enough of her. The first time they were married had been one of the best days of his life. But today, today felt like a dream come true.

"Thank you for loving me," Charlee said when the kiss ended, her eyes glittering with unshed tears.

"I can't help but love you."

*

If you enjoyed this book by Sharon C. Cooper,
Please consider leaving a review on any online book site, review site or
social media outlet.

Join Sharon's Mailing List

To get sneak peeks of upcoming stories and to hear about giveaways that Sharon is sponsoring, visit www.sharoncooper.net to join her mailing list.

About the Author

Award-winning and bestselling author, Sharon C. Cooper, is a romance-a-holic - loving anything that involves romance with a happily-ever-after, whether in books, movies, or real life. Sharon writes contemporary romance, as well as romantic suspense and enjoys rainy days, carpet picnics, and peanut butter and jelly sandwiches. She's been nominated for numerous awards and is the recipient of an Emma Award for Romantic Suspense of the Year 2015 (Truth or Consequences), Emma Award - Interracial Romance of the Year 2015 (All You'll Ever Need), and BRAB (book club) Award -Breakout Author of the Year 2014. When Sharon is not writing or working, she's hanging out with her amazing husband, doing volunteer work or reading a good book (a romance of course). To read more about Sharon and her novels, visit www.sharoncooper.net

Connect with Sharon Online:
Website: http://sharoncooper.net
Facebook:
http://www.facebook.com/AuthorSharonCCooper21?ref=hl
Twitter: https://twitter.com/#!/Sharon_Cooper1
Subscribe to her blog: http://sharonccooper.wordpress.com/
Goodreads:
http://www.goodreads.com/author/show/5823574.Sharon_
C_Cooper
Pinterest: https://www.pinterest.com/sharonccooper/

Other Titles

Atlanta's Finest Series

Vindicated (book 1)

Indebted (book 2)

Accused (book 3)

Jenkins & Sons Construction Series (Contemporary Romance)

Love Under Contract

Proposal for Love

A Lesson on Love

Unplanned Love

Jenkins Family Series (Contemporary Romance)

Best Woman for the Job (Short Story Prequel)

Still the Best Woman for the Job (book 1)

All You'll Ever Need (book 2)

Tempting the Artist (book 3)

Negotiating for Love (book 4)

Seducing the Boss Lady (book 5)

Love at Last (Holiday Novella)

When Love Calls (Novella)

Reunited Series (Romantic Suspense)
Blue Roses (book 1)
Secret Rendezvous (Prequel to Rendezvous with Danger)
Rendezvous with Danger (book 2)
Truth or Consequences (book 3)
Operation Midnight (book 4)

Stand Alones
Something New ("Edgy" Sweet Romance)
Legal Seduction (Harlequin Kimani – Contemporary
Romance)
Sin City Temptation (Harlequin Kimani – Contemporary
Romance)
A Dose of Passion (Harlequin Kimani – Contemporary
Romance)
Model Attraction (Harlequin Kimani – Contemporary
Romance)
A Passionate Kiss (Bennett Triplets Series)